Even Me

Even Me

Irvine Saint-Vilus

Divine Garden Press
www.DivineGardenPress.com

Published by Divine Garden Press, LLC
P.O. Box 371
Soperton, GA 30457
www.divinegardenpress.com

ISBN-13: 978-069225027
ISBN-10: 0692250328
Library of Congress Control Number: 2014944935

Cover Design & Interior Layout by Divine Lit Services
www.divinelit.com

To my mother, Mrs. Eternise Saint-Vilus and my brother, Stanley Saint-Vilus, without your continued love and support none of this would be possible.

Prologue

It had never been a fair fight between them. He was taller and heavier—angrier.

As a young girl, Daniela recalled the time when her father had come home after sleeping out the night before and her mother had questioned him on his whereabouts.

"Do not pester me, I am warning you. I am not in the mood for your talk."

"I have a right to question you," she responded, putting her foot down. "I am your wife, remember? At least that is what I am supposed to be, instead of all these other women you spend your time and money with."

He pointed a menacing finger in her face. "I am tired of your questions and I do not want to hear them. When you go to work and pay the bills then you can question me about what I do."

"I am not the one who requested to remain at home. That was your demand because you don't want me to be independe—"

She didn't get to finish her statement before the blow came to her face that sent her reeling back and grabbing her cheek from the pain.

Immediately Daniela heard screams and didn't realize they were coming from her own throat, which soon ached from rawness as she witnessed the scene.

Eventually, her mother came and took her by the hand. Moments later, they left and drove to her aunt's house. Daniela peeked at her mother who remained quiet as she drove; her cheek now discolored from the bruise her father had inflicted. Daniela wondered if it hurt and wanted to ask her mother about it. She wanted her mother to explain why her father acted the way he did. But she didn't say a word though tears silently fell from her eyes.

Daniela sniffled and in her heart she spoke to Jesus, asking Him to bring peace in the midst of a war that seemed to never end. But it was their story and remained that way for some time, the constant fights that slowly and steadily tore their small family apart. And she would always wear the battle scars across her heart, which years later would characterize her life.

Chapter 1

Micah's childhood potential had predicted a successful future, until disaster struck and altered the course of his life forever. Now he thought about some of his childhood antics and smiled with fondness. At age ten he demonstrated his entrepreneurial skills by masterminding a scheme where he and his brother, Mark, ventured out on their family estate in Charleston, South Carolina to catch all of the animals they could muster, including insects and reptiles; and then they set up an animal exhibit to showcase their findings. They managed to collect over one hundred dollars from their classmates (which they had to return after their parents found out) by convincing them that they were seeing ancient creatures from centuries ago.

He'd been reprimanded, of course, but he'd detected a smile of pride on his father's face as he doled out the punishment, which made Micah's own little chest puff out in satisfaction for making his father proud.

"That son of yours is something else," he heard his mother say after the incident.

"You have to hand it to him, that boy is smart." His father laughed boisterously. "You can bet he'll be ready to take over the family business when I step down."

"When you step down? I think he'll give you a run for your money right now."

Micah immediately began to dream about running Lambert Estates and making it bigger and better than they could imagine. His future was set...

Now Micah shook his head with regret, his smile replaced by a pained expression at the unpleasant memories that followed. He submitted to the stream of memories that often weighed him down and wondered how long he would continue to drown in the sorrows of his past. Sometimes the events were so fresh in his mind he could still feel his anger ripening at the injustice of it all and realized that the past remained a present battle.

With his hands plunged down deep in his pants pockets, Micah stood in front of the window in his home office and tipped his head upward toward the sun. Its intensity was dulled by the coolness of the weather, but he could still feel its beam warming his face and lightly penetrating his closed eyelids. Micah creased his lips into a terse expression. Though he was capable of determining darkness from light, he'd lost his vision years ago as a teenager after developing severe retinal disease of the eye, which prevented the back of his eye from sending light signals to his brain.

"It's not fair," he brooded. His anger at God was evident, and it produced a lack of faith he couldn't completely shake.

Even at 37-years-old Micah still couldn't fully accept his condition nor could he understand why God had dealt him such a difficult hand. He knew better than to be consumed by pointless reflections of what he'd lost, but he couldn't deny that they crept up on him anyway, reverting him back to the past and to the hurts associated with it.

There had been a point in Micah's life when he'd been content to be known as a Lambert. He'd come from a proud heritage of free blacks in Charleston, South Carolina, who'd managed to fight off the stronghold of oppression and make a name for themselves. They amassed a small fortune when his great grandfather had purchased his first plot of land and were now considered one of the most respected real estate entrepreneurs in the area. The family business flourished and was passed down through the generations.

Micah had been the potential heir to the Lambert real estate empire, but in the end he'd carved out his own path away from his family. But it wasn't the destiny he'd sought, and though he'd done well over the years in Charlotte, North Carolina, he still couldn't place enough distance between himself and the torn dreams of his past. Sighing, he withdrew from the window and trudged back to the massive mahogany desk that stood at the far end of the room and used his hands to guide him to his seat. He no longer had to count the number of steps it took to get from one end of the large room to the other since it was a daily sojourn; he practically lived in his home office where he conducted all of the daily operations of his business.

Micah tipped his head back against the headrest of the cushiony leather chair and surrendered to the unrelenting thoughts of his childhood. He recalled the day that'd altered the course of his life. He'd walked in on a private conversation between his mother and father, and as his parents talked, he heard what his eyes couldn't see, their frustration and disappointment; and he felt their rejection.

"I'm grooming Mark to take over the business," Morris told Ann Lee in a low and stolid tone. "He's the one who'll be taking over when I retire since we can no longer rely on Micah."

Micah's mother sighed. "Micah will be devastated, Morris."

"Do you think I like this?" his father asked, his voice rising. "But things don't always happen the way we expect them to. And right now we have to face the facts. Micah can no longer be counted on to run things because of his condition—"

"But how are we going to tell him that?" Ann Lee asked with a strain in her voice.

Micah, who'd been standing outside the doorway of his father's study, pinned his head against the wall and swallowed the sudden lump in his throat as he listened on.

"Besides," she added. "Are you sure Mark is willing to take on the position? The boys are close and he knows how much this means to Micah."

His father was silent for a few minutes, and Micah could imagine him bunching his lips to the side and leaning forward as he often did when he was in deep reflection.

"Mark has always wanted to prove himself to us and he's already indicated that he would be interested in taking on more responsibility in the business."

Gritting his teeth, Micah had heard enough. He turned around and walked away from the conversation and his family indefinitely. It was going to be too painful to witness Mark assuming the position that rightfully belonged to him as eldest son, essentially stealing his birthright, like Jacob had done to Esau, his least favorite story in the biblical Old Testament.

Micah stretched his shoulders back to relieve some of the burden of the guilt he carried around with him for having cut off all ties with his family. It'd been years since he'd spoken with them and with members of his extended family, except for his Uncle Joseph, whom he kept in touch with from time to time. Uncle Jo had been the only one who'd accepted him for who he was after Micah had lost his vision, and he'd given him encouragement when he'd needed it most. "Life's not over for you, son, just because you can't see it anymore," he'd said. Micah had had to replay those words in his mind each time he was tempted to give up hope that things would ever be right for him again.

Now Micah hovered over his desk and tried to get focused on his work. He shuffled papers about and sought a distraction from the upsetting memories that were treading too closely to the depth of the pain he still harbored inside but didn't want to acknowledge. For the most part Micah had done a pretty good job over the years of blocking out the thoughts that wanted to break down the barriers of his conscience, but lately they were becoming harder to ward off, and he found himself increasingly consumed by them.

"This is the way it has to be. This is the way they want it to be." He spoke aloud with conviction he didn't feel. Still it was enough to reinforce his pride and to swallow down the guilt brought on by his severed ties.

Though the guilt was gone for the time being, his anger remained and was exaggerated by a slight lift of his chin. Apart from a semblance of faith in the sovereign God who had shown him a vision and had given him the means to accomplish it, Micah's anger was what had fueled his ambition to obtain all of the success he now enjoyed as the owner of his own entrepreneurial business. This attitude was also what got him the respect of his peers and those with whom he did business, making them well aware that his blindness did not render him an imbecile, but rather he was quite capable.

Micah let another sigh escape his lips as he got down to work. He was doing research on the internet and used his screen reader to finish up a business article he'd been reading. He set that aside to focus on the papers in front of him. He passed his hands over the pointy surface of the documents to read them in Braille, which he'd learned in a specialty college for the blind. Currently, he was reading over the quarterly sales report for the business. He was an innovator and created technologically-advanced products and equipment for the blind community. Micah loved what he did, especially since it benefited others, including himself.

After a while, Micah got up and stretched, then he gripped the handle of his cane and headed out of the office space. He walked down the hallway and into his large, pristine, black and white kitchen and slid his hand across the dark, granite countertop until he'd made contact with the coffee machine and switched it on. By now he was very familiar with the schema of his massive two bedroom apartment in the fourth ward of Charlotte's uptown district and could maneuver around it with minimal trouble. Despite the varied accommodations and amenities that his complex afforded—the spas, swimming pools, fitness centers, and around the clock concierge services—it was the privacy that suited Micah. He let his hands be his eyes as he grabbed a bag of sliced bread from the pantry, and then opened the refrigerator door and pulled out a bottle of water, a container of turkey ham, and cheese to make a sandwich. He moved to place the items on top of the table in the dining room, but Micah banged his foot against one of the chairs which hadn't been pushed in its proper place and lost his balance. He toppled to the ground while the items in his hand scattered around him. He grabbed the offending chair and was poised to fling it across the room. Quickly coming to his senses, he dropped it and stood up. That chair wasn't the culprit. His anger was on account of a condition that would keep him permanently in the dark. He clambered past the mess, ambled toward the coffee maker, switched it off, and then stalked back to his office.

Chapter 2

Daniela was sitting in the midst of rush hour traffic and she grunted in frustration. Resigned, she sunk into her seat and braced herself for the long drive home. Soon she was far away in her mind to a place she often frequented whenever she attempted to make sense of the past and her bondage to it. Daniela traced her story back to a small, country town near Port-au-Prince, Haiti where she was born. Her earlier memories as a child were fond ones until economic times became increasingly difficult during the eras of dictatorship in the country, coupled with natural disasters that destroyed the land. Her father, who was a peasant farmer, started to feel the pressure of providing for his family. He grew more agitated each day, taking his frustrations out on her mother.

Daniela recalled him coming home one day and exploding when her mother asked him how his day had gone at work.

"Why are you asking me such a question?" he bellowed. "You already know how my days are. I work hard and still I come home with nothing. We cannot eat on nothing."

Her mother shrunk back from his reply. Later, he came to her and apologized and she accepted it. Years later, her mother continued to accept those empty apologies, even after moving to the United States, which

Daniela thought would make things better. Instead, the abuse escalated and the verbal attacks were accompanied by her father's fists.

Daniela shook her head in anger as she surveyed the traffic. Thankfully, it had picked up a bit and she was able to push on the gas petal and tried to push away those thoughts, which always managed to depress her.

Once she'd made it home, Daniela mumbled a short prayer of thanks to God before making her way into the kitchen. Then, with an exasperated sigh, she hoisted her heavy book bag onto the small wooden table and plopped down on one of the stiff-backed wooden chairs. She removed her shoes and gingerly massaged her worn feet; a tired grunt escaped her lips. Working, going to school full-time, and being actively involved in ministry at her church as Director of Ministry for the Needy, which helped the homeless in her community, made her feel overwhelmed. After the day's activities, Daniela often felt relief whenever she entered her small, cozy one bedroom apartment on the outskirts of uptown Charlotte.

Despite her hectic schedule, Daniela was encouraged in her efforts by a strength that could only be supplied by God, Himself. Her ministerial goal was to serve the Lord as a minister of His Word, and it took more out of her than she ever imagined it would. But it was also her calling, the path that she was destined to take, as well as the direction that she'd needed when she'd felt lost in the world, unable to move ahead and still stuck in the past.

Daniela turned her back on love, but she couldn't turn her back on God. She knew from childhood, largely due to her grandmother's influence, that God loved her and that He would always be with her. Once she'd made the decision to dedicate her life to Christ, she felt like she was being called to the ministry. This didn't sit well with her father who'd been pounding it into her head since childhood that she must become a doctor or lawyer. She recalled her conversation with her father after she'd made the decision to attend seminary.

"I am not the one who will be hurt if you throw away your life on foolishness, Daniela."

"This isn't about you, Dad. It's about what I feel in my heart God wants me to do."

"And what will you do with this degree? It will be useless to you," he bellowed. "You need to do something practical like become a doctor or lawyer. You have already wasted too much time."

Daniela resisted rolling her eyes. She had been hearing those strong-willed opinions for almost all of her life. Like many Haitian parents, her father made strong demands because he wanted her to aspire to become things that he could not.

"We were not all meant to be doctors and lawyers, Dad," she said in quiet defiance. "Some of us were called to live for God and to build His Kingdom."

"Called?" Her father scoffed. "Do you think God would call you to become something you were not meant to be? You are a woman, Dani, and this notion of becoming a pastor is foolish."

He shook his head and pointed his finger at her. "And even if you could do this, how will you use it to support yourself? You must come down to earth and live in the real world with the rest of us. And what about starting a family, you must think about that."

She turned away when he mentioned family because she didn't want him to see the look of disgust on her face. Daniela experienced what he'd done to his own family and wanted no part of it. Only her cousin Therese knew how much she actually wanted to be married to a good, Christian man. But her father's attitude toward her mother had created within her a strong distrust of men, in general.

Daniela recalled how her rejection of several potential relationships left her alone and filled with regret. Kevin Williams was a guy she'd known in college who'd seemed really interested in her. He'd tried to engage her in conversation several times, and finally made his intentions known one day.

Glancing up at him, she shook her head. "I'm sorry, Kevin. But I'm really busy with school and can't contemplate having a relationship with anyone right now."

"I understand you're busy with school and so am I." He gestured with his hands, his piercing eyes earnest. "But that shouldn't stop us from getting to know one another. We'll just schedule times to meet. And we can even study together."

Daniela kept shaking her head, her heart sinking because she could see the look of disappointment registered on Kevin's face.

Before he gave up pursuing her, he left her with words that would haunt her for years to come. "No one is an island, Daniela. I hope you realize that before it's too late."

Perhaps it was already too late in the love department, but Daniela didn't give up on her vocational aspirations, though for a time she'd lost her way. Grudgingly, she'd listened to her father's advice concerning pursuing a practical career and had enrolled in a nursing program Therese had recommended at a local university near their house. But soon after, she quit the program and took on meaningless work that had her going through the motions until her grandmother spoke the words that ignited the passion she needed to pursue her call to ministry.

"I can see that you are unhappy, Dani," she told her. "You will never be happy unless you are serving the purpose for which God has created you. If you know what it is then pursue it, my child. God will be with you."

Daniela had heard the words of affirmation that she needed. She enrolled in a seminary program out of state because she knew that it was also time to leave her father's house. She could no longer remain and be pressured into giving up her God-given dreams and aspirations for the future. Daniela left Miami, Florida for Charlotte, North Carolina, and found a job at a library to help pay for her schooling. And indeed the Lord was with her. Yet, it was difficult to dispel the doubts that were as rooted in the mind as the past. And it was the past that continued to make the future uncertain despite her conviction that she was doing what God wanted her to do.

Daniela took a quick shower and then made her way into the kitchen to warm up chicken soup for dinner. While waiting for the food, she took her book bag to her desk at the corner of the living room near the window and removed its contents. Sitting at the desk, she momentarily gazed out the window. The day was receding and a new one was on the horizon. She only wished she could move forward like the motions of time and not keep looking back at the failures and regrets of her past. But it was hard to move on when the past lurked at every turn.

Chapter 3

It was the beginning of November and there was a chill in the air. Daniela shivered as she walked briskly inside the main branch library in uptown Charlotte where she worked as a librarian assistant. Thankfully, it was much warmer inside the building, and she unzipped her knitted sweater. As she often did, Daniela took a brief tour of the premises to make sure that everything was in its proper place before getting down to work—booting up the computers and then sorting through the materials for shelving.

Soon after, she heard Frances' singsong voice ring out before spotting her coworker dashing toward the circulation desk. "I'm here, I'm here."

"That's progress. You're only fifteen minutes late this time."

"Not according to my watch."

She smiled at Frances, whom she called Free on account of her free-spirited personality. The two had developed a great working relationship when Daniela joined the library staff three years ago.

Frances snickered as she removed her leather jacket and shawl and folded them neatly underneath the checkout counter and then combed her fingers through her thick, auburn hair.

"Is our resident policewoman here yet?"

"No, not yet. And I don't think Erin would consider that a term of endearment, Free."

"I think our supervisor can handle the truth." She winked. "She's wound up way too tightly and you know it."

"Lord, please forgive her." Daniela glanced upward in mock exasperation.

"Still praying for the heathen, I see."

"That's right." She pointed at Frances and half-smiled. "And I won't stop either until you accept Jesus into your heart."

Frances groaned. "Please, it's too early in the morning for your preaching, Daniela."

Unaffected by her friend's statement, Daniela placed an arm around her shoulder. "All right, let's make a deal. Go to church with me one time and I'll leave you alone, at least for a good six months or so."

"Some deal." Frances shook her head and dispensed a wry smile. "We'll see."

"You're stalling, my friend," Daniela said.

She'd been trying to get Frances to attend church with her for a while, and refused to give up until her friend agreed. Though for now she'd have to forgo their conversation as library patrons were starting to arrive.

Before their checkout lines became too crowded Daniela decided to take time out to scan in some previously returned items and assess them for damages. While in the midst of sorting through DVDs she heard Frances whisper to her and looked up questioningly.

"Check this out."

Daniela followed her gaze and spotted a man standing near the automatic entrance doors with a white cane in one hand and the other in his pocket. He was dressed neatly in a burgundy wool cardigan sweater and tan slacks. He turned his head backwards and forwards to decipher his environment. People were trying to avoid bumping into him as they passed by.

"Good looking, if you ask me. Too bad he's blind."

"Free!" Daniela admonished sharply.

Frances shrugged and smiled. "Anyway, I'm already taken. But you, on the other hand, need to go over there and see if brother man needs some help."

"I don't think so." Daniela shook her head fervently. "I'm sure he brought someone with him to help him. Besides I'm busy with these returned items. And pretty soon we'll have customers lining up at the counter."

"I don't see anyone with him." Frances crossed her arms, a smirk on her face. "Come on, Dani, I'm sure there's something in that Bible of yours about helping someone in need."

"Now you're interested in what the Bible has to say?" Daniela said annoyed. She sighed, but reluctantly exited the counter and cautiously made her way toward the man. When she got close enough to him she stopped and announced herself to gain his attention.

"May I help you, sir?"

He turned in the direction of her voice with a relieved expression on his face. "Yes, I'm trying to find some books in Braille," he said, "preferably on the subject of business."

"I'm happy to say we are one of the few libraries that do carry Braille books, and we also have audio selections for added convenience. I can show you where they are if you'd like."

"Are you asking out of pity for the blind man?" he said with a hint of sarcasm.

Daniela faltered momentarily as she studied his frowned expression. "I was just trying to be helpful, sir," she said solemnly. "Please excuse me," she muttered as she turned away.

Her shoes made a low thud on the carpeted floor as she started to walk away. When she was several feet away from the man, she heard him clear his throat and say, "Please wait. I'm sorry."

Daniela turned around and stared at him with a slight frown on her face.

He rubbed the back of his neck sheepishly. "I guess I'm being overly sensitive. I could use some help if your offer is still on the table."

She hesitated and then nodded. "It is," she said. "Please take my arm."

He reached out and made contact with her outstretched arm, and they made their way to the back of the library. As they walked past the circulation desk Daniela averted Frances's probing eyes. But she couldn't ignore her sudden discomfort at feeling the light pressure of the man's hand on the bend of her elbow.

"Can you tell me your name?" he asked her.

"It's Daniela," she said stiffly. Then clearing her throat, she stole a peek at him. "And yours?"

"It's nice to meet you, Daniela. I'm Micah," he said.

They fell into an awkward silence as they walked the short distance to the back of the library.

"Thank you for offering to help me like this," Micah spoke up.

"It's–it's no problem. Uh–we're here," she eagerly announced and stepped out of his grasp.

Daniela clasped her hands tightly in front of her. "I'm sure we'll be able to find what you need in this section." She cleared her throat once more to remove the squeakiness in her voice. "Unfortunately, there aren't any Braille labels to alert you of what you need. That's something we need to implement in this library. I'll have to speak with my supervisor, Erin, about that." Daniela realized she was rambling and forced herself to stop.

To shield her embarrassment, Daniela instantly busied herself with finding the materials that Micah needed. She voiced some of the titles aloud to gain feedback from him.

He responded to her inquiries. And then he added off-handedly, "I used to be an avid reader but I barely can find the time to read anymore. So I don't get why I decided to stop in here looking for books."

"I enjoy reading also." Daniela seemed more at ease as they started a brief discussion on the efficacy of books. "It's a shame," she was saying, "that the young people today don't cherish books anymore like we do; they have too much technology to distract them nowadays."

"You're right about that," Micah said with a firm nod. "Between the iPods and iPads and Game Stations you wonder if they have time to sleep or even breathe."

Daniela giggled and echoed the sentiment. She was glad that she'd grown up in a period where computers and e-Readers were unknown entities. Though she could manage pretty well using the computer, it was still not second nature to her. And as far as book readers went, she couldn't foresee herself reading one without the added benefit of manually flipping the pages as though she were an active participant in the story rather than just a mere observer.

Micah tapped his cane against the shelf in front of him, carefully picked up one of the books, and opened it up. "So what else do you like to do besides read?" he asked casually.

"I don't have time for much leisurely activity, I'm afraid." Daniela picked up a few Braille selections and scanned through the audio books section.

"There must be something you like to do for fun," he probed.

"Actually, I used to enjoy the simple things, like going out for walks in the park or around my neighborhood but I haven't done that in centuries." She looked in his direction and wondered what it must feel like to not be able to enjoy a nature walk and to bask in the beauty of God's wonderful creation. "Do you have a favorite pastime?" she asked kindly.

"I had several at one time," Micah said with a wry expression. "But now what I really enjoy doing is getting away from the hectic work schedule I keep and spending some quiet time by this lake close to my apartment complex."

"That sounds very relaxing," she said.

"So I'm curious," Micah said after a brief pause. "When you go on these walks do you go alone, or do you have someone special to share them with?"

Daniela grew tense once more when she realized what he was asking. "I think I found some books you'd be interested in checking out," she replied instead.

"What would interest me is to get to know you, Daniela. It seems like we have a lot in common. Would it be possible to give me your number?"

She looked around in a slight panic. "I'm sorry but I can't."

"May I ask why not?"

She struggled to give him an answer, and Micah read into her hesitation.

"Let me guess, you don't give your number out to disabled men like me."

Daniela recoiled from his assertion and turned away. "I think we should head back now," she said with forced politeness. "I can check these items out for you at the circulation desk."

He nodded curtly. "I'm following your lead, remember?"

She escorted Micah back to the front of the library, the tenseness between them rendering them silent. She got behind the checkout register and ran his items through the scanner and then placed them in a cloth bag and handed it to him.

"I can walk you out if you'd like," she offered.

"No thank you. You've been very kind."

Daniela watched as he turned around and headed for the automatic exit doors and prayed that he wouldn't get run over by anyone along the way. As Micah held out his cane in front of him and walked out of the building, Daniela continued to see him long after he'd left the premises.

"You want to tell me what that was all about?" Frances had snuck up beside her and was now peering at her with her piercing, green eyes. "Did you finally meet the man who'll mend that broken heart of yours?"

"I'm not listening." Daniela smiled at her friend. But it wasn't only Frances she was trying to tune out. It was the sudden asymmetrical rhythm of that broken heart.

Chapter 4

Micah was still thinking about what'd transpired earlier in the day with the woman he'd met at the library, Daniela. He had to admit that her rejection had humbled him. He was used to women showing interest in him. Granted, he'd encountered most of the women he'd dated through business ventures or partnerships, and they knew of his competence and his successes. But Daniela had known nothing about him other than the fact that he was blind, which had led Micah to conclude that she'd turned him down for that very reason. He grew agitated to think that she'd been put off by his condition. He shook his head trying to fend off the thought.

Despite his desire to no longer ponder about the librarian, Micah reflected their interaction again in his mind. He could still hear the tense sound of her voice as she spoke with him. He wished he could have seen what she looked like. He'd noted her reserve and assumed she was the studious type, possibly with the glasses and the hair tied up in a ponytail or a bun.

Forcing himself to focus on something else, Micah meandered toward his bed and sat down, deciding to check his voicemail messages. He muffled a groan when he heard Claudia's message.

"Micah it's me, Claudia. I've been thinking about you, sugar, and thought I'd give you a buzz. I know you're not ignoring me, are you? We have unfinished business that we need to discuss, and I'm hoping we could go to dinner to talk. Give me a call okay? And don't delay. Bye."

For a time Micah thought Claudia was the answer to his prayers. They'd met at his lawyer's office where Claudia had served as one of the small business attorneys in the firm before going off to start her own private practice. She'd been the first to approach him.

He was sitting in the main lobby waiting to speak with his attorney when she walked up to him. "It looks like you could use a friend."

Micah turned to the sound of her voice and knitted his brow. "Excuse me?"

"I couldn't help but notice that you look a little down." Claudia sat down beside him on one of the chairs in the waiting room. "Can I get you anything? Water? Coffee?"

Micah was growing interested in the soft, raspy sound of her voice with every second they talked. "No, thanks. I'm waiting to speak with my attorney about a personal matter." He cleared his throat. "I guess you could say I'm not the happiest camper. I've found out that someone I trusted has been trying to steal from me."

He wasn't sure why he was being so candid with her, but she seemed so open and sincere and the truth was he did need a friend at the time.

"I'm sorry to hear that," she said.

Soon after, his attorney, Lee Langley, walked up to them ending their conversation. "Sorry to keep you waiting, Micah, but I see you've met our ace in the hole, Claudia Beauchamp," he said.

"Glad to meet you, Micah." Claudia took Micah's hand in hers and initiated a handshake. "Hopefully this won't be the last time we speak."

Soon they were moving in together and Micah and Claudia became inseparable. Then she began to push him about getting married.

"Things are fine the way they are now, baby," Micah said as he sipped his vodka tonic. "Why do you want to ruin a good thing?"

"Micah, I have an image to project if I'm going to further my career in the political arena."

"So this is about you."

She softened her voice. "No, sugar, it's about us, our future."

"Sure." Micah took another gulp of his drink, and the alcohol burned the insides of his cheeks and he winced.

"Will you stop drinking that poison for a second and answer me," Claudia exploded. "You're becoming a real drunk, you know that?"

"Well, there's an image for you." He shook his head and chuckled, which angered Claudia even more. She slapped the drink from his hand.

"I'm gone," Claudia said. "Let's see what you can do without me."

Now claiming a change of heart, Claudia wanted to give their relationship another chance. But Micah had serious doubts about turning back the clock and continuing a relationship that had been more hurtful than beneficial for the both of them. Still, he held on to a glimmer of hope that one day he would find the woman that would piece together the scattered puzzle that was now his heart.

Micah set the phone aside and bent forward, resting his arms above his knees and rubbing the corners of his eyes. He let his thoughts wander back to the encounter with Daniela once more. There'd been something about her that he'd liked. Perhaps it was because her modesty and sincerity had struck a chord with him. And yet there was complexity to her, a conflicting manner that sought to help, but also keep others at arm's distance. Micah understood her guardedness. Over time he had come across some shady people who'd tried to take advantage of him because they thought they could. But still he wished he'd succeeded in gaining her interest. Now Micah cringed. His behavior had been less than stellar after she'd declined to give him her number, and he was mourning that fact. There was a chance that he was wrong about Daniela's reason for turning him down. Regardless of the reason, Micah knew he'd have to go back to the library to apologize to her. He smiled to himself, unable to deny the fact that he was hoping for a second chance to make a better impression.

After taking a shower and getting dressed, he walked to the bed and sat down, fidgeting slightly. It'd been a full year now since he'd taken a drink but it was still a struggle. Shaking off the thought, Micah decided to pick up the Bible that was collecting dust on his end table. His fingers lingered over the Braille title. He used to pray and read the Word all the time while growing up. He also had to admit that God used him in some supernatural ways. Micah had been dumbstruck the first time God had spoken to him through visions.

The business he now owned had been a result of one of those visions. Sighing exasperatedly, Micah set aside the Bible. There was no use in opening it or turning its pages. The vision he really wanted, he didn't have, which was his physical eyesight.

Chapter 5

Daniela's vision was blurred as she sat in the middle pew of the empty church. It was customary for her to come to God's house when no services were being held and to spend time alone with Him. But today she was having trouble keeping her thoughts on the Lord because she was seeing her mother in her mind.

She leaned forward and put her head down atop the pew in front of her. The pain of her mother choosing to end her own life lingered, leaving Daniela to deal with the repercussions of her death, including the unanswered questions.

"Why didn't she just leave him?" Daniela asked her grandmother one day.

The older woman pursed her lips, her chubby cheeks jutting out sadly. "Because she did not know that she deserved better. When you do not think you deserve something more, you do not seek it out."

Gram patted the side of her bed, motioning for Daniela to sit down beside her. "Haitian women are proud, Dani. But we also have been raised to be submissive to our husbands and sometimes that means enduring bad treatment for a long time."

"Is that why you stayed with Grandpapa?" she asked carefully.

Her grandmother blew out a heavy sigh and nodded slowly. "I stayed for many reasons, and yes, that was one of them."

"I won't let that happen to me, Gram. I can promise you that." Daniela crossed her arms and pursed her lips.

"That is the reason why you must learn that you deserve better," Gram said with a gleam in her eyes. "So you do not make the same mistake."

Daniela knew her grandmother was right, but her words did not erase the fear of repeating the past. She wanted to believe that love and marriage were attainable for her, but she couldn't see beyond the fear evoked by the memories. Sitting up, she thought about the encounter she'd had with the man she met at the library, Micah. His interest in her had been both flattering and unsettling. Admittedly, Daniela had been curious about this man and felt a tinge of regret for not reciprocating his interest.

"No one is an island," she whispered aloud. "Then why am I so set on being alone?"

"Are you all right, Sister Daniela?" Pastor Moses Sanders' voice rang out as he entered the sanctuary.

Daniela looked up and spotted him standing at the front of the church stage near the podium. His dark leathery skin, peppery mane, and beard spoke of a tough life that'd produced wisdom beyond her years. She was grateful to have this man of God as her mentor.

"I'm just doing a lot of thinking, Pastor Sanders." She tried to smile. "I didn't know you were here."

"I came in about half an hour ago to finish up some work," he said. "I saw you in here praying and I didn't want to disturb you."

Daniela nodded. "I'm glad you keep the doors to the sanctuary open all the time. It helps sometimes to be alone with the Lord in His house."

"I can attest to that." He nodded.

She glanced away from Pastor Sanders's inquisitive look. She knew he wouldn't pressure her to speak with him if she weren't willing or ready to do so.

Pastor Sanders cleared his throat. "Well, take all the time you need. I'll be in my office for a little while longer. Whenever you're ready to leave let me know and I'll walk you to your car."

Alone once more, Daniela closed her eyes and prayed for healing from the past, which continued to influence the decisions she made. It made her fearful of failure in ministry and in finding the elusive love she sought from a godly man. She prayed for God to direct her steps as she sought to put off the old self and to put on the new.

Chapter 6

Micah sat behind his desk and attempted to study the proposal for his latest design. Normally, he was on top of things in all areas of his business and had no problems making decisions, like his cost analyst's estimates for their latest project, the Can-Do-Cane. But right now he couldn't concentrate long enough to make sense of the documents in his hands. Growing frustrated, Micah flung the pages aside, stood up, gripped his cane, and made his way into the kitchen. He resigned himself to what was really on his mind, the vision of Daniela he had formulated.

Micah walked into the kitchen and opened one of the cabinet doors near the sink and gripped a glass from the bottom shelf to fill it with orange juice. He'd hired both a housekeeper and an organizer to help him keep things in order in the kitchen and throughout the apartment. The neater and tidier everything was, the better it was for him to find anything and everything he needed. Right now he was appreciating the fact that every item was stored away in an uncluttered and recognizable fashion. Each drawer or cabinet was labeled in Braille to alert him of their contents.

Micah let his hands be his guide as he retrieved the carton of juice from the refrigerator. He ignored the juice after he'd poured it, and instead, leaned up against the kitchen countertop. He had already concocted a vision of what this woman looked like and who she was inside. She was pretty with soft brown skin and soft and silky, shoulder-length hair. She was reserved and strict, but also kind and generous. She was tall and slender with large eyes that displayed sadness that was attached to the soul like a birthmark fastened to the skin.

Micah was able to perceive what others couldn't and in their short conversation he'd detected so much in the sound of her voice. He knew that if he was able to look into her eyes he would see her life's story written in them, her heartbreaks and regrets and somehow he'd felt a connection with her because he understood that story all too well. Could she be the one he'd been waiting for? Micah wasn't certain but he knew he needed to find out. And the best way to do that was to talk to her again.

He went back into his office and sat down behind his desk to work, but it remained the furthest thing from his mind. Micah checked his Braille watch and moments later called his driver and asked him to bring the limousine around. With his cane tapping in front of him, he made his way to the elevators and down to the lobby. Inside the car, he sat at the edge of his seat and ruminated over what to say to Daniela to somehow convince her to trust him.

Micah braced himself for another possible rejection from Daniela as he slowly made his way inside the library. After his first visit he'd made it a point to calculate the steps to the circulation desk. Tentatively

Micah was heading in that direction, but he stopped midway hoping that she'd somehow notice him as she had before. He perked up his ears and listened to the noises in the library. To his left he picked up on hushed tones and conversations, and to his right he heard a baby crying.

"Can I help you?" someone said to him.

Micah turned in the direction of the high pitched voice. It didn't belong to Daniela but he was content to hear it anyway and be noticed.

"Yes," he said. "I'm looking for someone; I believe she works here."

She squinted at him. "I might be able to help you with that. I'm Frances," she said. "Why don't you tell me who you're looking for?"

"Yes, her name is Daniela. Unfortunately, I don't have a last name."

"And can you tell me what you want with Daniela?"

Micah furrowed his brows curiously, and then he smiled with discernment. He extended his hand. "My name is Micah. You must be a friend of Daniela's. Am I right?"

"Good guess." She shook his hand firmly. "She's out to lunch right now," she said. "But I guess it's all right if you wait. She should be back in about fifteen minutes or so."

"Thanks." His smile broadened. "Where should I park myself?"

"To your right and about two feet away is a square wooden table and some chairs. You can grab a seat there and I'll let her know you're here when she gets back."

Micah followed her directions, sat down at the table, and waited, sowing interest into a woman he barely knew.

Daniela walked through the automatic doors of the library in deep thought. She got behind the checkout counter and got right to work, mechanically gathering the returned items and setting them up on a cart to be shelved.

"How was lunch?" Frances asked her from behind.

"I think you were right when you said that we should petition Erin to extend our 30 minute lunch to an hour," she said, smiling.

"Sounds like a plan," Frances said. "But right now there's someone else you need to speak with first."

"Who's that?" Daniela frowned.

"Micah, your blind prince." Frances smiled as she pointed Daniela to where Micah sat waiting for her.

Though Daniela's heart sped up at seeing Micah, she tried not to show any expression on her face, especially since she spotted her friend watching her intently. "I don't know what he wants," she said with a shrug. "It's too early to return the items he'd checked out the other day."

"Well, why don't you go on and find out."

Though she nodded and made her way toward his table, Daniela grew apprehensive as she recalled their first encounter. What could he possibly want from her, especially after he'd accused her of treating him unfairly? Still she found herself smoothing down the front of her blouse and skirt along the way as though Micah could see her.

"Hello, Micah," she said guardedly as she approached the table where he sat. "I heard you were waiting to speak with me."

"Daniela." He stood up. "Please excuse my unannounced visit."

"How can I help you?"

"Can we sit down and talk for a few minutes?"

"I really have to get back to work."

Micah sighed and nodded. "I can tell I'm not your favorite person right about now." He paused. "I don't want you to have the wrong impression of me. I know I came off a bit too strong when we met, and I apologize for that. But I genuinely wanted, or I should say want, a chance to get to know you. And as you can probably tell I don't handle rejection very well."

Daniela's heart softened toward him as she sensed his sincerity. She pulled up the chair across from him and sat down. "I wasn't trying to reject you, especially not for the reason you think."

He pulled back his chair also and sat down, leaning forward and intertwining his fingers. "I was hoping you'd say that."

She smiled thinly. "I know what it's like to be judged by appearance, and I don't want to do that to someone else."

"Then prove it and allow me to take you out to lunch," he said, smiling. "Unless you weren't being truthful just now."

She hesitated and Micah quickly sought to convince her to accept his invitation by saying, "I'm interested to learn more about you, that's all."

Daniela bit the corner of her lip and squinted at Micah. She was intrigued by him too, and her curiosity was stronger than her fears, though she had to be cautious because although he was blind, Micah was still a member of the male species, and not to be easily trusted.

"How do I know you're not some serial killer," she said with a hint of humor. "You never know these days."

"Come on, you can hurt me quicker than I can hurt you for obvious reasons," he said with a smile. "But think about this. When we first met, you had no idea who I was but you still helped me." He placed his elbows on the table. "I know it's a lot to ask for you to trust me, but all I'm asking is for a few minutes of your time. Can you give me that?"

He was making it hard to say no. Praying she wouldn't regret it, Daniela heard herself agreeing to meet with him.

"There's a sandwich shop a few blocks down the street called Sasha's Deli," she said. "I guess we could meet there for a few minutes at around five if you'd like."

"Great, I'll be there." He scooted out of his seat.

"Would you like me to escort you out?" she asked as she stood to her feet.

Micah's easy smile became tight. "No that's all right."

Micah sat in the backseat of his limo brooding. He reflected on his coarse reaction to Daniela's kind offer to help him back at the library a little while ago. He would have gladly taken her up on her offer had he not been so preoccupied with the thought that she'd pity him and think of him as some invalid who couldn't fend for himself. It was important to Micah that Daniela knew he was quite capable of caring for himself, especially since he feared that she was counting his condition against him, though she denied the charge. Still, even though he hadn't wanted to appear weak and disabled in front of her, he hadn't wanted to come off like a brute either.

"Are you all right, Mr. Lambert?"

Micah turned his attention to his limo driver, Ben, an elder gentleman who'd been Micah's faithful employee for over two years. Micah liked the fact that he was a man of few words, but the things he said were always ripe with wisdom.

"I might've just blown my chances with this woman because I can't keep my cool," Micah responded.

"What makes you think you blew it?"

He bent his head down and rubbed his palms together methodically. "I didn't want her to help me because I thought she was feeling sorry for me."

Ben grunted.

"That's all you got, Mr. Ben? No words of comfort?"

He chuckled. "You may not want to hear this, sir," he said. "But how about letting her decide what she thinks instead of you deciding for her."

"So in other words, I jumped the gun."

"Maybe so," Ben confirmed.

Micah nodded, once again appreciating the wisdom of his limo driver. "Maybe you're right."

He was considering how to approach the conversation he would have later with Daniela when he received a phone call. He didn't hesitate to answer it when the screen reader program on his phone announced who the caller was.

"Hello, Uncle Joseph," he said. "It's been a while. How are you?"

"I have bad news, Micah," the older man said, his tone flat. "Mark was attacked earlier today by some thugs who wanted to rob him. And when he resisted, one of them shot him at close range."

A moan rose up from the pit of Micah's stomach. He cupped his hand over his mouth to stifle it. "How is he?" he managed to ask.

"He was taken to the emergency room at Charleston General Hospital, and right now we don't know the status of his condition. But it's a delicate situation." Joseph's voice tapered off and he cleared his throat. "Listen, Micah, I hope you'll make the drive out here. Your brother needs you right now."

Micah anchored his elbow above his knee and held his head in his hand. He couldn't think about what he needed to do right now. It was enough of an effort to formulate words.

"Call me as soon as you know anything, Uncle Jo," he said hoarsely. "I'll be in touch." Then he hung up before his uncle could get another word in.

"Why?" Micah shook his head and whispered through gritted teeth. "Please, if You can hear me, God. Don't let him die. Don't let Mark die."

Later, inside his apartment, Micah couldn't escape the awful silence that forced him to conjure up the worst of scenarios regarding Mark's condition. They resurfaced and filled him with past regrets; the images of happier times between him and his brother he'd stashed away in the storehouse of his mind.

Micah sat heavily on the couch in the living room. He tried to contact his uncle to get an update on Mark, but there was no answer. He tried again a second and third time with the same result. Sighing, he stood up and walked over to the living room window.

"How can I go back?"

Chapter 7

Daniela sipped her latte drink and tried to swallow down her embarrassment for having been stood up. She had gone to the deli shop to meet Micah like she promised but he never showed up. Now she felt like a fool for having trusted a man she didn't even know.

She cringed when her cell phone rang and saw Frances' number showing on the caller ID, knowing that she wanted the details surrounding the meeting that never took place. Daniela had told her about seeing Micah that afternoon as a precaution in case something should happen to her. Now she almost wished she hadn't.

Sighing, Daniela answered the call. "Hey, Free."

"Okay, enough with the small talk. Tell me about your date with the blind prince."

"It wasn't a date and nothing happened, literally. He never showed up."

"You mean brother man stood you up?"

"You said it," she said dryly.

"I wonder what could've happened. He seemed to really like you, Dani."

"I don't know, and I was foolish for going in the first place," Daniela said dismissively. "I'd better go, Free. I have a lot to catch up on. I'll see you tomorrow, okay?"

"He's the fool, kiddo, not you," Frances voiced with conviction. "See you tomorrow."

No sooner had she hung up the phone, it rang once again. Glancing at the caller ID, Daniela cringed for the second time. It was her father. They hadn't spoken in weeks. She contemplated on whether or not she should continue that pattern. But in the end she answered the call on the fourth ring.

"Hello, Dad."

"W bliyé fanmi'w, Dani. You have forgotten about your family," her father huffed in Haitian-Creole, their native language. "You may not care for me. But you should at least call to see how your grandmother is doing."

"Why? Is Gram all right?"

There was a slight pause from her father's end, which alarmed Daniela. She repeated the question with more urgency.

"She fell down in the bathtub and broke her hip," he said in a monotone voice. "But she is home now and she is not in too much pain."

Daniela was already in tears. "Why didn't you tell me sooner?"

"If you called more, you would know what is going on with your own family."

She bit her lip to avoid arguing with him. "I will take some time off this week to come and see her," she said after a pause. "I'll let you know what day I'm coming."

After she hung up the phone, Daniela flung herself down on the living room couch and covered her face with her hands. A scream escaped her lips, originating from the pit of her stomach. "I cannot lose Gram too," she sobbed.

Micah had woken up in the middle of the night with cold sweats. He got up to change his undershirt. It'd occurred before—jolting out of sleep and gasping for breath as though he were suffocating. Now Micah sat back against the couch in the sitting area of his room soaking up the frigid air circulating from the vent overhead. His head drooped drowsily but he could not sleep. Instead he listened to the faint sound of rain drizzling outside. It procured images of him and his brother, Mark, playing board games in the family estate to pass the time on the summer days when there was a downpour and they'd had to stay indoors. But that was years ago, prior to losing his vision and losing the close bond that they'd once shared as brothers.

Micah pushed himself up out of his seat, the sad reality of Mark's condition dawning on him once again.

In the stillness of the night, Micah could hear the accusations in his head. *This is your fault. If you had been the brother he needed you to be this wouldn't have happened.*

Right now he wished he hadn't made a conscious decision to stop drinking completely. Initially, the alcohol had done the job of keeping the troubling memories at bay, but when it'd started taking over his life, Micah knew he needed to stop.

Now dealing with Mark's condition, as well as his own role in it made the destructive extracurricular habit appealing to Micah again, which meant that he needed an intervention and fast.

"God help me," he sobbed aloud. "Why won't You help me?"

Micah gripped his head in his hands. "It's bad, son." Micah recalled Uncle Joseph's words when they finally spoke. "The doctors think there may be some permanent damage from the bullet that penetrated his skull and brain. Now he's in a coma and they don't know when he'll come out of it."

Micah grabbed hold of his cane and marched into the kitchen. He pulled open the cabinet door and searched for his escape, the bottle he knew he should've gotten rid of a long time ago. He twisted the cap open and drew the bottle to his lips with his hand trembling.

"If You can hear me, God. I need You to show up right now or I'm going to down this whole thing. I swear." He gritted his teeth and waited, turning his face backward and forward expecting what, he didn't know.

"Yeah, that's what I thought," Micah blurted out. "You weren't there before, and You're not here now."

He tilted his head back and gulped down the liquid with it dribbling down his chin. Then dropping the bottle, he shook his head and sobbed.

"No . . . no . . . no," he yelped.

With a loud cry, he hurled the vodka bottle across the room.

Chapter 8

Although Daniela was not enthusiastic about having to face her father, the dreaded meeting was inevitable since she had to go see her grandmother, who didn't seem to be getting any better. Late Friday evening, Daniela started her long trek from Charlotte to Miami, only pausing to fill up her gas tank. At 9:00 a.m. on Saturday, she pulled up to the driveway of her father's house in the northern part of the city. It had remained practically the same over the years; some properties were more run down than others, but most were still in good shape, and the one story houses lined up neatly along the neighborhood streets.

Before stepping out of the car, Daniela bent her head and uttered a desperate plea as she fought against the nostalgia of being back to the place where her past took center stage.

"Thank You, Lord, for Your grace, love, and mercy. I come to You now to ask for healing for my grandmother and peace with my father."

Grabbing her small suitcase, Daniela trudged up the walkway toward the house. She unlocked the front door with her spare key and stepped inside of the brick house she'd called home for most of her life.

Daniela shut her eyes momentarily and reminisced about the temporary euphoria she'd felt when they first moved into their one level, three bedroom home.

"Does this home belong to us?" Daniela had asked her mother with wide eyes.

"Yes, Dani." Her mother smiled. "It is ours."

It had taken a long time before they could move into their own home when they first arrived from Haiti. Until then they lived with her Aunt Sylvia and her family. Those times brought good and bad sentiments. They were good for Daniela who enjoyed a close relationship with her extended family, especially her cousin Therese who was around her age. But they were bad because her father grew increasingly angry and frustrated at the difficulties of providing for a family and not finding the means to do so. He took his frustrations out on her mother. Eventually he found a job as a mechanic and they were able to buy this home, but the relationship between her mother and father only got worse, going from verbal attacks to physical violence.

Daniela shook her head before the bad memories began to seep into her mind and make her remember why she'd stayed away for so long. The house was quiet. She surveyed the eclectic furnishings in the living and dining rooms, and then made her way into the kitchen. Immediately, tears brimmed to the surface of her eyes as she imagined her mother sitting down at the kitchen table and burying her face in her hands from wounds that wouldn't heal. Daniela walked over to the spot where she'd seen her lying down on the ground, the evidence of her body now long gone, but the memory a stain that could never be removed.

"You're here," she heard him say.

Daniela whirled around and came face to face with her father. She nodded her head, certain that her voice would not hold up if she spoke. They had stopped displaying affection long ago, and Daniela didn't go to her father to give him a hug or a kiss. She was certain he wasn't expecting that from her anyway.

He turned away from her quizzical stare and plunged his hand in the pockets of his blue trousers. "Your grandmother is resting in her room if you want to see her."

Her scrutiny of her father showed a man who had aged much too quickly. His hair was almost gray; the bones of his face were prominent; and his dark brown eyes were sunken and lifeless. Her heart stirred within her and she sensed a feeling she hadn't expected— regret over how things were between them. Glancing downward at the tiled floor, she searched for something to say to him to ease the tension but words escaped her. And after moments of agonizing silence, she walked stiffly passed her father and went to see her grandmother.

Daniela knocked on the door and then peeked inside before entering the room. Her grandmother was lying on her bed groaning slightly. She tiptoed over to her, knelt down, and gave her grandmother a hug and a kiss.

"Dani," Gram said in a deep, groggy voice. "You're here."

"Yes, Gram. I had to come and see you." She spoke to her grandmother in Creole, their native tongue, because Gram didn't speak English. Sitting down near the edge of her grandmother's bed, Daniela asked, "How are you feeling?"

"I feel like my body is broken into a thousand pieces."

Daniela smiled and patted her grandmother's hand soothingly. "Thank God it's only your hip that's broken."

Gram chuckled lowly. "I am glad you are here, Dani. Have you seen your father?"

Daniela's smile faded as she nodded.

Her grandmother sighed heavily. "I know you are still angry with him. I pray that one day you will be able to forgive him in your heart."

Me too, she thought as she stood up. "May I get you anything, Gram? Did you already have your breakfast? Did you take your medication?"

"Yes." Her grandmother moved gingerly on the bed and groaned once more. "Do not worry about me, sweetheart. Your father has called to have someone come here often to help me and to check in on me."

Daniela shook her head dubiously. "Maybe I should come back permanently to help out," she said while anxiously surveying her grandmother.

"You cannot leave your school, Dani," Gram said with a shake of her head.

She sighed. "Gram, I could always transfer if I need to. Also, there are new technologies now that allow people to take their classes over the computer."

Gram reached out and put a shaky hand on top of Daniela's. "I want you to finish what you have started. That is how you can help me."

Daniela didn't reply. She sat with her grandmother for a while and watched as the older woman fell into a light slumber. She stood, bent forward, and kissed her grandmother lightly on her forehead. "I'll be back to check on you soon," she whispered.

As she left the room and shut the door behind her, the thought of moving back to Florida took a foothold in her mind. Walking inside her childhood bedroom, she sat on the canopy bed and looked around nostalgically. It still had many of the things she enjoyed as a child on display, like her dolls and stuffed animals, and her favorite childhood books. Those were what made living in the midst of violence and chaos more bearable, in addition to her prayers. Daniela felt heaviness at the pit of her stomach as she considered the decision she had to make. Returning to Florida would allow her to help her family, but it would also bring her back to a past she was trying so desperately to escape.

Chapter 9

It was a massive one level factory building that he'd had renovated to replicate the vision he'd had for starting his business. Now Micah walked inside the large brick building that he owned and stopped midstride to absorb his surroundings.

"What's happening, Mr. L?" Ace McMahon greeted him. A good-natured, talented sketch artist, Ace had become one of Micah's most valuable assets, and Micah relied on him to bring to life a lot of his inventive ideas. Ace was also the only person he considered a friend outside of work. His Christian morals made him trustworthy, which was the most important attribute an employee needed to possess in Micah's view.

"I wish you'd stop calling me that, man," Micah said in a surly tone.

"I always call you that in the office." Ace frowned. "Are you all right?"

Micah pushed forward, heading to his office, while Ace trailed behind him. Micah rounded his desk and plopped down.

"What's up, man?" Ace asked.

"I've got a lot on my mind." Micah began gathering paperwork and activated the screen reader on his computer. "And before you start, I don't want to hear any of your God talk this morning."

Ace didn't say anything and waited for Micah to speak.

"I messed up," Micah said finally. He raised his palms and let them fall on his desk and sat back in his chair. He rubbed his face with his hands. "I took my first drink in over a year, a whole year of sobriety down the drain because I was too weak to say no."

Ace took a seat across from Micah's desk. "You're not the only one who's ever messed up, Micah. We all mess up sometime. It's the staying down that's the real problem."

"I should've had more willpower than that." Micah gritted his teeth.

"Look, man. Whether you want to hear it or not, that's what God is for. He's strong when we are weak. You've got to turn it over to Him."

Micah turned his face away. "I got some work to do and so do you."

"I guess I'll leave you alone then."

Micah heard the hint of hurt in Ace's voice and grew contrite. When he heard the door close, he tilted his head back against the headrest and sighed aloud. Ace didn't deserve his disdain but Micah was too consumed by his own anger to apologize.

On his way back from the site, Micah attempted to contact his uncle to get the latest news on Mark's condition. These calls always made him nervous, and he tried not to anticipate the worst as he waited for Uncle Joseph to answer the phone.

"Hello," his uncle said after what seemed like a long time.

"I was hoping you had some good news about Mark. But I'm guessing from the sound of your voice that that's not the case."

"No, it's not," his uncle voiced grimly. "You know, you could find these things out for yourself, son."

"Uncle Jo, you know as well as I do that being there will only stir up strife."

"But what took place in the past shouldn't matter right now," Joseph said earnestly. "What should count is supporting your brother in his time of need."

"I wish things could be different, Uncle Jo, but they're not. All they'll see is the past when they look at me, and I can't make them accept me."

"They're still you're family, Micah, whether you like it or not. Besides, you can pray about what's happening between you and Mark. That's what I've been doing since this whole ordeal started."

"It'll take more than prayer, Uncle Jo. It'll take a miracle," Micah commented lowly. "And I'm starting to think that God's no longer in the miracle business."

"There's no benefit to talking like that, son," his uncle responded gravely. "He's the same yesterday, today, and forever."

After hanging up the phone, Micah shook his head dubiously, though his uncle's words continued to reverberate in his mind. Could his relationship with his family be resuscitated like the dead coming back to life? At some point he knew he'd have to go and visit Mark. But deep down he knew he wasn't ready to face his family—at least not yet. For now, he'd have to take his uncle's advice and pray from a distance. He decided to go to the one place that always seemed to bring him some peace—the lake near his apartment building. It reminded him of the times he spent at the beach when he was growing up.

Now Micah stepped out of the car and breathed in the zesty, rainy scent that was coming up from the water down below. He needed no assistance in journeying down the cemented walkway that led to a bench on the grassy areas near a fence. He sat down and placed his elbows on his knees. He turned his head backwards and forwards, trying to discern the beauty of the scene before him, the stillness of the water, the occasional singing of the birds overhead, and the faint voices belonging to people nearby. But there was also a sense of solitude that quieted the unsettling thoughts in his brain and allowed him to think things through.

Though it was a cool afternoon Micah barely noticed as he sat back against the hard back of the wooden bench and took in a deep breath and then exhaled. Without reserve, he spoke words from his heart, wishing Someone up there *was* listening. Now he was asking the question that kept plaguing his mind since news of Mark's attack. "How do I face them?" he whispered. "How do I go into that hospital room and pretend that everything is all right between them and me?"

Micah pursed his lips at the deafening silence. But it was in the midst of it that he verbalized his worst fear, the fact that his brother was lying in a hospital bed fighting for his life, and the guilt of playing a part in what was happening to him. Maybe if he had been a better brother and hadn't practically abandoned Mark, this wouldn't have happened.

Micah stood up and walked to the fence that blocked the path to the edge of the lake. His mouth quivered with emotion. Suddenly he dreaded the seclusion he normally sought and now wished he had someone there with him who could hear him out and offer words of encouragement and comfort. He thought of Daniela. He was certain that she was someone he could trust. Micah thought about her voice and the image of her he had etched in his mind, and possibly his heart, ever since he met her weeks ago. Micah had to continue to figure out a way to get her to trust him. But it wasn't going to be easy, especially after he'd stood her up on the day he'd found out about Mark. Though it'd been for a good reason, Micah hadn't had the opportunity to speak with her and to apologize for not keeping their date. When he'd gone to the library to speak with her once more he'd been told that she'd be off for the rest of the week. Sighing, Micah only hoped that she would allow him access into her life and maybe build a trusting relationship that could lead to something more down the line. But right now he wasn't sure about anything and was burdened by more questions than answers. He turned around and traced his steps back to the limo where his driver was waiting to take him back to his apartment.

Chapter 10

Daniela saw her father staring across the room at the pictures on the mantle in the living room and debated on whether or not she should approach him. In the end she spoke up and asked if he was all right.

"I am fine."

She sighed quietly, assessing the haggard expression on his face and gathering that he was far from "fine." That'd always been his way, to hide his pain or any emotion behind his pride. After her mother died he'd shut down emotionally and had refused to display any feeling, which angered Daniela. Now looking at her father, she saw clear cracks in his armor. He was slowly disintegrating under the weight of his own internal struggles, and she wished she could reach out to him. But how? And would he let her?

Slowly, Daniela walked into the living room and sat opposite her father on the couch. She glanced down at her hands, and her throat felt constricted as she sought to verbalize her feelings.

"It's been so long since we really talked, Dad. Is there anything you want to talk about?" she said.

He turned and looked at her blankly. Then he turned back to the pictures on the mantle. "I had forgotten how much you looked like your mother."

Her mouth parted slightly in surprise to hear him bring up the subject of her mother, which was usually a topic that was off-limits where he was concerned. "I miss her," Daniela ventured to say, her voice a whisper.

He got up and placed his hands in his pockets, his head hanging down. "You do not have to tell me what you think of me, Dani. I see it in your eyes every time you look at me. You blame me for everything that happened, and you are right." He turned away. "I'm going to work this afternoon and I won't be home till late. Let your grandmother know."

Daniela remained on the couch for a long time, trying to digest her father's words. She did blame him for a lot of what happened. But she realized that though she'd already lost her mother, she was also losing her father. She needed to find a way to bridge the distance between them before that happened.

"Lord, please help me," she mouthed quietly. "Please, help us."

Feeling the weight of her burden, she kept her eyes shut and continued to pray in her heart, even as she got up to check on her grandmother.

Daniela brought Gram some soup to eat, and then checked her blood pressure and sugar level as the nurse's aide had shown her to do. When Gram settled down for a nap, Daniela went into her own room to catch up on some much needed school work, which she'd brought with her. But it was difficult to concentrate. She walked to the window across from her bed, recalling the times she'd stared up at the sky from this very spot on many sleepless nights, when her mother and father would have their arguments. Or worse yet, when the silence was so thick it'd scare her. She'd prayed to God for answers then, and she found herself praying to Him for answers now concerning moving back to Florida to help her family.

She reasoned that besides school and work there was nothing keeping her in Charlotte. Curiously, an image of Micah surfaced in her mind. She frowned, wondering why she would even think about a man who had stood her up, though he'd been the one to ask her to meet with him. And though she'd been curious to know who this blind man was and what he'd wanted, Daniela reasoned that it was for the best that they didn't get to speak. He was certain to be a complication that she didn't need in her life. What she did need was to distance herself from her thoughts and from the sadness that pervaded this house like a lingering fog. She exited the room and made her way to the front door. Her father had retired to his bedroom. Sighing she shut the door behind her and got behind the wheel of her car. She needed to get away.

Before Daniela even rang the doorbell of the townhome where her cousin lived with her parents, Therese opened the door and pulled her into a tight hug. Daniela held on to her cousin and drew comfort from her warm embrace.

"I can't believe you're here. It's been way too long, Dani."

"I know." Daniela nodded and smiled ruefully. "I've missed you too, Tess."

Therese was a natural beauty with a heart-shaped face and soft, delicate features that stood in stark contrast to her strong-willed personality.

When they parted, Daniela inquired about her aunt and uncle who were both at work. She glanced about the house that'd been like a second home to her growing up. Not much had changed. The oversized furnishings made the space appear smaller than it was but it also gave it the homey feel that Daniela always enjoyed.

"I hope you're hungry," Therese told her. She led the way into the kitchen where she fixed up two bowls of her mother's scrumptious stew. They carried their meals along with iced lemonade drinks to Therese's bedroom.

"I know you're worried about Gram." Therese studied her sad expression.

Daniela nodded and picked at her food. "She doesn't look too good."

"She'll bounce back. She always does."

"I pray you're right." Daniela set her bowl aside and took a sip of her drink. "But right now I want to talk about you. What's new?"

Therese put her bowl down as well and began gesturing excitedly with her hands. "What would you say if I told you that your cousin is getting married?"

"You're getting married?"

Therese nodded, her smile stretching from ear to ear.

Daniela listened to her cousin's account of the proposal with outer joy but inner turmoil. Daniela was rejoicing with her cousin while mourning for herself, for she was certain that she would never get to this place in her life when she would become somebody's bride.

Therese stopped talking suddenly, a sympathetic grin lining the corners of her mouth. "I know what you're thinking, Dani," she said. "But you're wrong. It's going to happen to you too. Just believe that God will give you the desires of your heart."

"I gave up on that idea a long time ago, Tess."

"This is me you're talking to, Dani. I know how much you want to be married and to have a family of your own someday."

Daniela didn't respond, and Therese shook her shoulder playfully. "You have to stop letting what happened between your parents dictate what happens to you, Daniela," she said. "You are not them. You are your own person with your own path in life."

"You're the one who's wrong, Tess." Daniela shook her head. "I came from them. And sometimes I fear my own self, because I wonder if I will become the monster that my father was, or the victim that my mother became."

"God did not give us the spirit of fear, remember Pastor?"

Daniela smiled despite herself. "Thanks for the reminder," she said dryly.

"No problem."

"I guess we'll just have to wait and see if that ever happens. But in the meantime, I'll help you with your wedding day as much as I can."

Chapter 11

Claudia had just completed a successful asset transfer for her client, which meant a nice paycheck for her. Playfully, she patted herself on the back, taking great pride in being the successful attorney that she was, never downplaying her capabilities. Modesty was not one of her greatest attributes.

Admittedly, she could've easily coasted through life, being the daughter of a famed judge and a renowned model and actress. However, she wanted to make a name for herself on her own terms. Perhaps that was the reason why she and Micah had bonded in the two years that they'd been together. She could understand what drove his passion to succeed because she possessed it also—the need to be the best regardless of what other people thought, said, or did.

Claudia was used to getting anything she set her mind to, which was why she was growing increasingly frustrated at Micah's reluctance to her request to give their relationship another chance.

She sighed as she entered her large, three bedroom condo. She immediately felt better as she glanced about her luxury flat, with its high, vaulted ceilings and large open-concept living room and kitchen. She kicked off her heels and slipped onto her cushiony sectional couch.

Her thoughts went back to Micah again and she frowned. *What happened to us, Micah?*

However, Claudia knew exactly what'd happened. Micah wouldn't comply with her goal to establish herself as a powerhouse in the business world, which would fuel future political ambitions. His financial success and good-looks had made him her ideal mate, despite his blindness, which had become a slight hindrance that she was willing to deal with. But she wouldn't put up with his growing drinking habit, which put her future in jeopardy.

"You're throwing away the best thing that ever happened to you," was one of the last things she'd said to him.

"You're the one who changed the rules, Claudia." He turned in her direction, with drink in hand. He took a sip and winced from the potency of the alcoholic beverage. "Now you have a high list of demands and ultimatums." He shook his head. "What you see is what you get."

"People grow up, Micah. Why don't you?"

In the end she turned her back and walked away, certain that he would fall to pieces without her; and even more determined that she could find someone to replace him and continue pursuing the life she always dreamed of for herself.

Yet Claudia discovered that Micah hadn't fallen into ruin without her. According to mutual acquaintances, he seemed to be doing better than ever in his business, and he was no longer drinking.

"It's time to rekindle the romance, Micah, sugar," she whispered.

Claudia got up and headed straight into the bathroom to run a bath in her jetted tub. Nothing could relax her more that to soak in that tub for a bit. When it was simmering and soapy just as she liked it, she stripped and stepped in, carrying a glass of red wine and her phone. With a smile on her face she looked up Micah's number and pressed the talk button. It was time to make another plea for reconciliation and she refused to take no for an answer.

"What can I do for you, Claudia?" Micah frowned as he spoke into the telephone.

"Hello to you too, sugar. And you already know the answer to that question," she said in a silky voice that sought to cajole him. "You can give me another chance, Micah. I think we owe it to ourselves to try again, and to get things back to the way they used to be between us."

"We've been through this, Claudia." His voice took on a stern undertone. "Things have changed and they can't go back to the way they used to be." Micah sat down on the living room couch and impatiently tapped his foot against the polished wooden floor. "And let's not forget that it was you who made the decision to end things between us, and not me."

"But I made a mistake." She pouted.

He sighed and leaned forward anchoring his elbows above his knees. "It wasn't a mistake, Claudia." He softened the tone of his voice. "It was for the best, and we both know that."

"Can I come by so we can talk about this in person?"

"That's not a good idea," he said adamantly.

She chortled. "You have to admit we had some good times together, Micah."

"Yes, I agree. But I remember the bad times too."

She sighed. "I won't give up on us, sugar, if that's what you're thinking," she said, her tone resolute, then it faltered. "Have you met someone else—is that why you won't give us a chance?"

"I'm not going to discuss that with you, Claudia."

"So there is someone."

Micah shook his head in frustration and rubbed the back of his neck. "Listen, I'll talk to you later, okay?"

After he got off the phone with Claudia, Micah went into his office to get ready for a telephone conference call with some investors regarding sponsorship for an upcoming product. Once it got under way he settled back in his chair and tried to remain focused. He didn't miss a cue to invoke the importance of his products and his track record for success.

Micah's shoulders relaxed and his expression was one of utter concentration. He nodded as though he were in the same room with the people with whom he was speaking. "I'll do that," he said. "I'll have the documents forwarded to you as soon as possible."

However, once he ended the call, Micah's confidence faltered as he began to think about his personal trials; the guilt for not visiting his brother, and the yearning for the love of a good woman who could be at home in his heart.

Chapter 12

Daniela placed her order and took a sip of coffee eagerly while she waited for her bagel and cream cheese sandwich. She'd driven home from Florida the night before and was still recovering from the lack of sleep.

"Daniela?" Micah said aloud.

She turned around and gawked at Micah, the blind man who'd stood her up, standing behind her, waiting to place his own order. He was being escorted by a man in uniform who looked like his driver.

"I'm sorry if I'm mistaken," Micah added, "but I thought I recognized your voice while you were placing your order. Am I right? Are you Daniela from the library?"

What do I do? Daniela thought. She could ignore him and walk away, which he deserved for standing her up. These were the times when she hated the call as a Christian to take the high road and *to do to others what you would like done to you*, rather than to do to others what was done to you.

"Hello, Micah. Yes, you're right, it's me, Daniela." She was already jetting toward the exit door. "I hope you have a nice day."

"Please, wait," he said with an anxious expression on his face. "Can you spare a few minutes. I'd really like to talk to you. Please?"

She tilted her head back in defeat and slowly turned around.

Micah knew that this had to be more than a mere coincidence. He had taken a break from work to get a bite to eat and decided on a whim to go by the deli where he was supposed to meet Daniela and now there she stood, gawking at him he was certain.

"I'm sorry about not showing up for our lunch appointment," he told her now. "I had a family emergency that called me away. But I'm hoping we could talk now if you have some time to spare."

He could envision the debate going on in her mind and only hoped it worked out in his favor.

"All right, Micah," she said finally. "I can spare a few minutes."

He smiled his thanks. "Do you mind leading the way?"

Micah felt her hesitation when she cleared her throat and then grabbed hold of his extended hand and escorted him to a table near the storefront window, while Micah's driver, Ben, retreated back to the limo.

"I always say grace," she said pointedly when they'd taken their seats.

"I do too," he said. "Please go right ahead."

He smiled at her silence and was certain she wasn't expecting that kind of response from him. He bowed his head and Daniela prayed a short but ardent prayer of thanks for the food.

"So you're a believer?" she asked.

"You can say that," he said, "though I haven't always lived my life as such."

"I don't think any of us can without His help."

She watched him in fascination as he ate methodically, his movements deliberate and unhurried. Micah slowly gripped his cup of coffee and took a sip and then he set it down in the same spot to know where to pick it up again when he wanted it. When he searched for a napkin she pushed one toward him discreetly. With a nervous knot in the pit of her stomach she waited for him to broach the topic of their meeting.

"Please don't take this the wrong way," Micah said. He wiped his mouth with a napkin. "But I'd like you to describe yourself. You have an unfair advantage of knowing exactly what I look like but I can only guess your looks." He smiled boyishly. "Besides I came up with an image in my mind and I want to see if I was right."

She touched her cheek in embarrassment and hesitated before speaking. "I guess you could say I don't follow normal conventions. I'm medium height, and slim in size." She stopped and glanced downward. "I have milk chocolate brown skin; I wear an afro; and I'm told I have large, thoughtful eyes." She smiled shyly. "So how did you make out? Is that the picture you had in mind?"

"Actually, it's even better than I envisioned."

"I'm flattered," she said.

He smiled. "So are you from around here, Daniela?"

"No." She considered not saying anymore, but Micah's silence prompted her to add, "I'm originally from Haiti but I grew up in Miami, Florida."

"Do you still have family in Haiti?" he asked interestedly. "What made you decide to move to Charlotte?"

She glanced away even though Micah couldn't see her look of trepidation. Musingly, Daniela watched the gaiety of a little girl as she bounded up to the deli counter, pointing at what she wanted while her parent or guardian trailed helplessly behind her. The scene made her smile and cry inside because she knew no such innocence. As a child she'd been stripped of the joyous freedom of youth, and she'd been running from the culprit ever since, which had taken her as far as Charlotte, North Carolina. But instead of disclosing the truth about her place of refuge, she stated vaguely, "I came here in search of new opportunities."

"Please don't think I'm grilling you," Micah said with his palm raised. "But like I said before, I just want to get to know you better." He paused and she watched as he pressed his lips together pensively. "What I'm saying is I'd like us to become friends and then see where it can go from there."

Daniela squirmed in her seat. What was she supposed to say? That she would rather not start a relationship that she was certain would be doomed to failure?

Her lengthy silence caused him to frown. "Am I asking for too much?"

"I don't do much socializing, Micah." She turned her head away with thoughts of Kevin Williams' rebuke reverberating in her thoughts. *No one is an island, Daniela.*

She watched as his demeanor changed.

"I guess I got my answer," he said coolly. Micah stood to his feet. "I won't be bothering you again."

Daniela shut her eyes and her heart bled. Had she gotten so self-centered that she was letting her own personal struggles overtake her duty as a Christ follower to fellowship with other believers? Micah was asking for friendship, not marriage.

"I'm sorry," she said. "I'm pretty cautious about things, and about people, that's all."

Micah sat down once more. "I understand that. But you have to be willing to trust someone sometime, and coming from someone like me who needs to be extra careful about who he deals with, that's saying a lot." He offered a smile. "So the way I see it, you and I can help each other. We can learn how to trust by building a friendship with one another."

"So this is a case of misery loving company?"

He chuckled. "Yes, something like that."

Daniela glanced toward the storefront window of the shop and watched as the sun's rays broke through the lightly tinted glass and reached them from where they sat. "How would we begin this friendship?" she asked distantly.

"How about starting off by telling me something people don't normally know about you."

She looked at him and thought for a moment before responding. "All right. Not too many people know that I'm concluding my coursework to become a pastor," she said in a slightly defensive tone.

He digested the news and nodded impressively. "What made you decide to go that route?"

"It's my calling," she said with less guardedness. "But some people don't believe that because I'm a woman. That's why I make it a point not to judge a book by its cover, because I know how that feels."

Micah grunted as he set aside his food and propped up his elbows on the table. "So are you ready for the kind of scrutiny you will face?"

"Sometimes I think I am," she said. "And then other times, I'm not so sure."

"Like I said, we're a lot alike. I know how it feels to doubt yourself because others can't see what God is doing in your life." He reached for his coffee cup and took a sip from it.

She studied his sober expression. "Please tell me something about you, Micah."

He was silent for a brief moment as he pondered what to say. "I lost my vision at the age of fifteen," he mused. "And now I design products for the blind; a case of the blind leading the blind if you'll pardon the pun." He pruned his mouth as though he'd bitten something distasteful.

"I think that's great," she said kindly. "You're doing something to help other people."

His frown lines ebbed and a smile was playing on his lips. "My motives aren't that pure, you know," he said. "It's been a profitable business."

"Well, you can only continue to do good if your business continues to be successful, right?"

"You're very diplomatic." His smile broadened.

"Should I take that as a compliment?"

"You should."

She gasped as she noticed the time displayed on the clock hanging on the wall of the deli shop. "I have to go."

"Is everything all right?"

"I lost track of the time." She got up out of her seat and began to gather up everything on the table. "I have to head to class now."

Reluctantly Micah stood up. "I'm sorry you're running late, but I'm not sorry we spent this time together."

"I enjoyed our talk too," she said shyly.

Micah gripped the handle of his cane. "So what's the verdict? Are we friends?"

"Yes, I'd like that," she said, glancing up at him.

Micah nodded in satisfaction.

Chapter 13

It was the end of a busy workday and Ace stopped by to chat with Micah before heading home. He plopped down on the chair across from Micah. "How's it going?"

Micah shrugged while keeping his focus on the papers in front of him. They were quiet for a short while and then Micah cleared his throat and popped his head up, a look of contrition on his face. "Listen, I didn't mean to blow up at you the other day; I guess I still have some anger issues to sort out."

"Yes you do, but I won't hold it against you."

"Thanks," Micah said with a wry smile. He sighed and leaned back against his chair. "I told you about my brother. I know I need to plan a trip to Charleston to go and see him but I've been reluctant to do it because I don't want to have to deal with the family drama."

"I know how stressful that can be, for sure."

"I keep thinking that maybe if I'd been around, this might not have happened, you know?"

Ace shook his head. "Don't blame yourself for something that was beyond your control, my man."

"Then why do I feel so guilty?"

"When you feel guilty you have no peace and that's the work of the enemy." Ace narrowed his eyes. "Now God convicts us to do what's right. Though you had nothing to do with what happened to your brother, God may be convicting you to go see him because He wants you two to reconcile. He does say in His Word, if you are offering a gift at the altar and then remember that your brother has something against you, go and reconcile with your brother first, and then come and offer your gift."

"Maybe you're right."

"Don't get me wrong," Ace said. "Things don't always work out for the best."

Micah furrowed his brows, giving Ace his undivided attention.

"Now take my brother, Rondell," Ace said. "We chose separate paths in life. He chose the wrong side of the tracks and got involved in the drug scene, and that cost him because now he's serving jail time."

"Wow, you never told me about this."

"It's not something I like to talk about. I still care for my brother and pray for him every day. But he refuses to see me because he doesn't want me to talk to him about turning his life over to God. Ultimately, he's going to have to make that decision on his own."

"It's hard to give up old habits," Micah said distantly.

"True," Ace said.

"Like women, for instance." Micah got up and walked over to the window behind his desk. "I'm still thinking about my ex even though she and I were poison when we were together."

"That crazy ex you told me about?"

Micah had to laugh at his friend's reference to Claudia. After they became friends, Micah and Ace swapped stories about each other's exes to see who could top whom, and Micah won with the stories he shared about some of Claudia's antics.

"Yup, that's her. She's been calling me lately and wants to reconcile." Micah shook his head.

"All I can say is don't do it."

Micah walked back to his seat. "There is this other woman who's been occupying my thoughts lately." He leaned forward in his chair and furrowed his brows. "She is the opposite of Claudia."

"Just remember that he who findeth a wife findeth a good thing, my brother." Ace stood up. "Speaking of which, I better head on out of here before the wife starts calling me nonstop to see what's keeping me out so long."

"Say hello to Tonya for me." Micah smiled.

"Will do," Ace said.

Once he was alone, Micah reflected on Ace's words and had to admit that his friend was speaking words that resonated with wisdom. But was he ready to listen?

Micah wanted to get to know Daniela to see if she was the one he was waiting for; the wife that Ace talked about. Micah had gotten Daniela's number from their previous meeting and decided to give her a call to see if they could get together on a Saturday afternoon.

"Hope I didn't catch you at a bad time," he told her while leaning forward with his elbows propped up on the desk in his home office.

"No." She cleared her throat to hide the nervousness in her voice. "How are you doing? And how are things with your family?"

At the mention of his family Micah's smile faded. He stood up and paced a short distance from his desk. He didn't want to think about Mark lying in that hospital bed and his guilt at not having gone to visit him. Thinking about it always relegated him to a past he wasn't ready to face.

"It's still a touch and go situation," he said evasively.

"I'm sorry," she said. "But don't give up and keep praying. God always works things out for the good of those who love Him."

He tilted his head upward listening to the conviction in her voice. He frowned once again sensing her conflicting attitude between matters of faith and matters of the heart. But he decided to curtail his curiosity, at least for the time being.

"Thanks for the encouraging word, I needed to hear it."

"No problem," she said.

There was a moment of silence that passed between them. He tried not to lose his confidence as he propelled himself to reveal the reason for his call.

"I was hoping you weren't too busy this afternoon, Daniela," Micah uttered. "I'd like us to do some more talking. And maybe you'll have more encouraging words to share with me."

There was more silence coming from her end. "I'm not sure I'd be good company; I wouldn't give you my undivided attention since I'd be thinking about the art and science of Hermeneutics and word pronunciations in Greek and Hebrew."

"I know school can be tough." Micah's shoulders sagged slightly. But he popped his head up. "But like you said earlier you can use a break. How about we go for some fresh air; I'll even treat you to ice cream for being such a good, devoted student."

She giggled. "That's hard to pass up."

"Great." He nodded approvingly. "How about I pick you up in half an hour? We can go to Creamy Goodness Ice Cream Shop."

Daniela hesitated. "Is it okay if we meet at the ice cream shop instead?"

"In other words, I'm still untrustworthy," he said with a hint of humor. "All right, we'll do this your way."

Creamy Goodness was located near the center of uptown. His driver parked near the entrance, and Micah leaned against the door of his limo and waited for Daniela. His head was tipped downward as he listened closely to the sounds of laughter from children playing nearby. Immediately, his mind reverted back to the day he and Mark and their father had gone on a fishing trip together when they were young boys. Micah almost laughed out loud as he thought about their competing to see who would catch the most fish; their enthusiasm so over the top that he and Mark nearly toppled out of the boat. But just as quickly the happy memory faded and was replaced by the sobering reality of the present tragedy. He gritted his teeth against the dull pain in his heart.

"Hi, Micah," Daniela called out as she approached him. "I hope you haven't been waiting long."

Micah felt his spirits lift considerably as soon as he heard her voice. "I'm a patient man," he said, smiling and issued a slight shrug. "Shall we go inside?"

He extended his hand toward her. Daniela hesitated before taking hold of it and placing it at the nape of her elbow.

She seemed to relax when they started talking about their favorite flavors and toppings. Micah noted her enthusiasm, which was akin to that of a little girl. He couldn't help but to compare her love for the simple pleasures to Claudia's expensive and elaborate style. They were like night and day.

After they'd placed their order, Micah took out his wallet and removed a folded bill from the pocket and extended it over the counter toward the young cashier who took it from him and rang up the order.

Once they'd taken their seats at a table in the relatively empty shop, Micah discerned that her mind was filled with unasked questions about his blindness.

"Ask me," Micah said suddenly, a small smile playing on his lips. "I know you're curious about how I knew what to give to the cashier. Am I right?" he said.

"I am curious," she confessed.

"I fold up the bills differently which allows me to pinpoint their value. Also, most of the time I can tell how much the bill is by the feel of the currency; coins are easier since they come in various shapes and sizes. But paper money takes more practice." He paused and turned his face away and blew out a breath. "I don't mind answering questions when someone really wants to know and understand and not prejudge. What I have a problem with are judgmental people who make assertions about your abilities because you lack something that they take for granted every day. And somehow they think you less of a person for being different from them."

His anger was palpable and she let him express it with no interruption. Once he became aware of his changed mood, he calmed himself and gave her a rueful smile. "I'm sorry, I didn't mean to go off like that," Micah said.

"It's okay." He could hear her dipping her spoon inside her butter pecan ice cream and swirling it around in her cup. "Though being a woman is not a handicap it can feel that way sometimes," she said quietly. "In many instances you're not placed on an equal footing with the men, and that goes for ministry as well."

"It must be hard to be respected in a male dominated industry." He nodded. "You're made to feel like a second class citizen, and I can empathize with that."

"It's a good thing that as believers our true citizenship is in heaven where we're regarded equally," she said with a sober ring in her voice.

"I agree, Pastor Daniela."

She giggled. And their conversation took on a lighter tone as they enjoyed their ice cream.

"This is good," Daniela said content, as she savored another bite of the creamy treat. "I'm glad you talked me into it."

"Something tells me you're not thinking about homework now," Micah said, teasing.

"Okay, you got me. All I can think about right now is this cup of decadence in my hand. And I have you to thank for that."

"I'm happy to serve." Micah smiled and then cautiously added, "You know, we could do this again tomorrow evening. Of course I'd insist that we have dinner first."

Daniela shifted in her seat. "I'm sorry, Micah, but I can't."

He set his cup down and didn't say anything, but his expression conveyed his disappointment.

"You see, I have to attend a church meeting tomorrow night," Daniela explained. "I'm involved in a ministry to help the needy people in our community. We're trying to put together a food and clothing drive to distribute to the homeless, especially with the holiday season coming up.

"Maybe we can go out some other time," she added with a mixture of sadness and relief in her voice.

"Okay, let's make it next Saturday night," Micah persisted with an amused look on his face. "Or is there a meeting on that night too?"

"No," she said with a soft chuckle. "Saturday night will be fine."

"Great." He sat back and smiled openly. "Now about this ministry you're involved in. It sounds like a noble cause and I'd like to help out. I have tons of clothes I don't need, and I can even make a financial contribution."

"You don't have to do that."

"But it's already done," he said, smiling once again.

Chapter 14

It was for this purpose that Daniela had gone to seminary in the first place, to become a purveyor of God's Word, wasn't it? She wasn't so certain anymore as she sat at her desk and forlornly stared down at the unfinished sermon in her hand. If she was called to preach and teach God's Word, why was she hesitating to do so now? And why was the road so difficult?

She set the paper down and got up from the desk to take a much needed break. Daniela pondered the various reasons why she was sinking into the mires of doubt about her calling. For one thing, it had always been a point of contention between her and her father, who didn't support her decision to enter the field of ministry and especially becoming a pastor.

Daniela also encountered resistance from church members who believed the Bible forbade women to preach. She frowned as she thought about the conversation she was meant to overhear between two women in the church who opposed the pastor's decision to make her an associate pastor upon graduating from seminary in the coming year.

"The Bible specifically says that women are to keep silent in the church," the woman sitting behind her at the church service whispered loudly.

Her friend affirmed her statement with a grunt.

"I mean the Word of God is clear," the first woman said. "Women are to learn in quietness and in full submission."

"That's right," her companion accented, "says it right here in first Timothy chapter two, verse eleven."

Pursing her lips, Daniela could feel the pesky eyes of the women, who were sitting behind her, boring into her as they continued to talk about her. Unwilling to sit idly by any longer, she turned around and squinted at her foes, two longtime members of Bethel Baptist Church.

"Do you know that the first evangelist in the Bible was a woman?" she asked rhetorically. "I suggest you read Luke chapter two, verse thirty-six about a prophetess named Anna who was the first person to go and spread the word about our Lord and Savior, Jesus, immediately after His birth."

With that she turned back around and wore a stolid expression, her concentration in the service gone. Yet she did gain a sense of satisfaction for halting the gossipy duo behind her who was stunned into silence by her unexpected outburst.

Feeling the weight of her doubts, Daniela knelt down in front of her chair and began to pray. "Lord, I believe You called me to do this work. And I'm supposed to preach my first sermon to the congregation on Sunday." She prayed with fervency, her hands gripped together tightly, her brows kneaded together in anguish. "But I'm beginning to doubt that I can do it, Lord. What if I can't do it?"

In the depths of her soul she recalled a biblical passage from Philippians 4:13 and it brought a smile to her face and quelled some of her fears. "I can do all things through Him who gives me strength. Thank you, Lord," she said.

Getting up, Daniela returned to the sermon manuscript and continued to labor on for the rest of the afternoon.

Before the Wednesday night prayer service started, Daniela entered the sanctuary and spotted the Ministry for the Needy treasury secretary among the crowd of people. She walked up to her and happily handed her Micah's monetary donation, which he'd given her as he'd promised, and watched as the older woman's eyes lit up. Then she tiptoed to her own seat as service was already in progress. She bowed her head to pray before standing to join the rest of the congregation while they sang a well-known hymn. Daniela immediately relaxed as she clapped her hands and moved to the rhythm of the upbeat instruments, namely the drums and guitar of the church band. She glanced about her and saw a sizeable group gathered tonight, especially for a weeknight.

After the song of worship everyone sat down and the offerings were collected. She waited in anticipation of her favorite part of any church service to begin—the dispensing of the Word of God. Pastor Sanders was a powerful preacher; he felt every word that he uttered, gestured grandly to make others feel them to, and never tried to detain the move of the Holy Spirit to exact His will in the service.

When he took to the podium, however, it was to introduce a guest preacher who was unbeknown to

Daniela. He was a young man, medium height and build, with prominent features that demanded attention, especially his hawkish nose.

"I'm happy to be here among God's people tonight," the young preacher began with a ring in his high-toned voice. Then he proceeded to preach a stirring message that moved the audience, including Daniela. He spoke of surrendering to God and letting Him mold and shape you into the image of Christ through the fruit of His Holy Spirit.

He concluded the message with a pleading invitation to come to Christ. Daniela was happy to see some people responding to the altar call and surrendering their lives to Christ. When the final prayer was cited and the benediction given, the congregation dispersed. Daniela waited to speak with Pastor Sanders.

"How is your grandmother?" he asked as soon as he spotted her.

"She's doing better, thank God." She hugged her Bible and hymnal against her chest when she noticed the young preacher, who stood a short distance away, looking in her direction.

"Glad to hear it," Pastor Sanders was saying with a look of concern. "As soon as you told me that she was sick, I haven't stopped praying for her."

"Thank you, Pastor. I appreciate all the prayer and support."

"And how are you doing?"

"I'm doing fine—"

From behind them they could hear the visiting pastor clear his throat. Pastor Sanders turned and motioned him to come forward. "There's someone I want you to meet, Sister. He's the young anointed pastor who preached here tonight, Mason Goodwin. He comes to us from Good Hope Baptist Church."

Mason Goodwin took hold of her hand and peered at her with unflinching eyes. Daniela had to glance away. After she'd greeted Pastor Goodwin and commented positively on his sermon, Daniela focused her attention back on the elder pastor.

"I wanted to confirm my participation in Sunday's service with you, Pastor Sanders."

"Yes, Sister, it's a go. You are definitely on the program."

Mason Goodwin looked back and forth between them and frowned curiously. Pastor Sanders filled him in.

"Sister Daniela will be preaching her first sermon this coming Sunday," he said, smiling. "And one day she will be one of our associate pastors here at Bethel."

She watched the younger preacher's surprised expression.

"Is that right?" he said. "Things certainly have changed."

Daniela squirmed under the scrutiny of the young Mason Goodwin, and she sought to get away from him as soon as possible.

"Well, I'd better get going," she said. "You gentlemen have a good evening."

Chapter 15

Micah's exasperation continued to show on his face long after he'd left the investment firm. He'd gone there to meet with some top investors who'd shown interest in sponsoring his latest design, the Can-Do Cane. But as soon as he'd walked into the suite, Lorraine Jennings, the firm's secretary, had made her intentions toward him known, brushing past him flirtatiously on several occasions while he waited to meet with the investors.

Once upon a time Micah would've responded to her obvious passes with flirtations of his own. But that time in his life had passed and he didn't want to turn back the clock. He pursed his lips as she lightly grazed his back with her hands and placed a hand on his shoulder.

Leaning against his ear, she whispered, "Why don't we get together tonight?"

"I'm flattered, Ms. Jennings. But I'll have to say no."

Micah had left the investment firm feeling relieved, gratified by his moral victory which eluded having to pay for a mistake called Lorraine Jennings. Now on his way home he ruminated over his biggest blunder yet, which was Claudia Beauchamp, the woman who'd walked out on him without the courtesy of an explanation. At the time he'd been receptive to Claudia's neediness. She'd made him feel like a complete man and not some invalid, and that had been as important to him as breathing. So when she left him, she nearly cut off his circulation. Thankfully, he'd bounced back. And he didn't want to make the same mistake twice no matter how much Claudia begged and pleaded with him about giving their relationship another try.

Besides he had someone else on his mind now. The more time he spent with Daniela, the more he was growing fond of her. He still wasn't sure where their friendship was headed but he realized that his heart was becoming invested and he didn't know whether to cheer it on or to mourn that fact.

He reflected on their most recent date. When Daniela agreed to go out with him on Saturday night, Micah wanted to make it a memorable occasion, so he'd took her to an amusement park. She'd told him that she was surprised, just as he hoped she would be.

"I wanted to bring you here because I thought it would be fun and relaxing."

"It's been years since I've been to an amusement park. It reminds me of the last time I went to the fair in Florida with my cousin Therese." Daniela laughed out loud. "She and I competed to see who could get on the most rides without getting sick. Needless to say, she won."

She fell silent and Micah sensed her apprehension.

"Are you...sure about being here?" Daniela asked. "I wouldn't want you to get hurt, Micah."

They were walking together on the grounds of the park and he stopped suddenly. He could hear the chatter of people all around him, smell the fragrance of foods that were permeating the air, hear the swooshing of the rides and the music coming from the loud speakers, and he could imagine the vibrancy of colors that were splashed all over the park. He frowned deeply at the injustice of not seeing it all.

Unable to swallow back the tinge of bitterness that peppered his response, Micah growled, "Blind people aren't invalids, Daniela. We're not confined to our homes never to venture out again."

He could feel her stiffen up against his hand as he held on to her arm and he sighed. "Listen, Daniela. I just don't want you feeling sorry for me."

She didn't reply for a short time, and he grew anxious in his heart. *Had I blown it?* he thought.

"I *will* feel sorry for you after we've been on twenty or so rides and you can't stand up anymore," she said with a hint of humor in her tone.

"What have I gotten myself into?" he smiled in appreciation. Then patting her hand, he added. "Please lead the way."

Micah didn't remember when he laughed so much as they went from ride to ride and feasted on the foods. But what he remembered most was how she cared for him, guiding him with every step they took, and he felt like he could trust her completely with his life . . . and his heart.

When his cell phone rang Micah snapped out of his thoughts. "Please give me some good news, Uncle Joseph."

"The news is good for a change, son," the older man said. "He's still not conscious but his vital signs are better and they've upped his condition from fatal to serious and stable. He's on the eighth floor now, room 8115."

Micah angled his head upward and mouthed a thank you to God. "That's great," he said with a crack in his voice. "I know he will make it through this."

"Your visit is long overdue, Micah."

"Have they even asked about me?" he voiced defensively.

"That's not the point," his uncle said. "This is no time for pride."

Micah rubbed the edge of his temple, annoyed by his uncle's stern rebuff. "I thought you'd understand my position, Uncle Jo."

His uncle sighed. "I do, Micah. But I also know that if anything was to happen and you weren't there you'd never forgive yourself."

After hanging up the phone, Micah considered praying, but quickly dismissed the idea. He knew his faith wasn't where it needed to be and he needed someone who could rally with him. He needed someone there beside him when he finally made the trip to visit Mark, and someone who would be willing to pray for Mark's healing. The one person who came to mind put a smile on his face.

The phone rang and Daniela answered willingly, her heart pounding to see his name written across the phone screen. "Hey, Micah, how are you?"

They'd remained in contact since their previous meetings and she found herself looking forward to his calls and their conversations, which were always pleasant.

"Hi, Daniela," he said. "Listen, although this is short notice, I was hoping we could meet this evening. There's something important I wanted to speak with you about."

"Is everything all right?" she asked with a frown.

"It's better if I explain in person. Can I come by your place?"

She didn't respond, suddenly rubbing the edge of her temple anxiously.

"You know you can trust me by now, right?" Micah asked.

"Yes, I know." But he'd never been this close to home before, threatening the wall of defense she'd carefully constructed around herself, which unnerved her. Quickly, she gave him the address to her apartment building before she changed her mind. And then Daniela waited in agony until he arrived.

When her phone rang once more, her heart skipped a beat as she answered it. Micah was downstairs in front of her building.

"I'll be right down," Daniela said.

Drawing a deep breath, she opened the door of her apartment and then climbed down the cemented staircase to where Micah stood. He looked nice, casually dressed in a turtleneck sweater and jeans.

She cleared her throat. "I'd invite you up, but it's late."

"I'd be surprised if you did." Micah smiled.

"There's a bench not too far from here," she said. "We can sit there and talk."

Micah nodded and extended his hand toward her. Instinctively, she gripped it and circled it around her arm. She led them to a brown, wooden bench situated to the side of the building. She let Micah's hand go as they sat down together.

Micah rubbed his hands together methodically and hung his head down. "I told you that I had a family situation but I never told you what it was about."

She listened intently, watching the gloomy expression on his face.

"It's my younger brother, Mark. He was victimized recently in a robbery attempt. One of the thieves shot him and now he's laid up in a hospital bed in a comatose state."

"I'm so sorry to hear that, Micah," she voiced sadly.

"I need your help, Daniela." He shifted his body toward her. "I want to go visit Mark and pray for him, but I need you to go with me. I see your faith and I believe God will hear your prayer."

She didn't say anything and felt her heart thump against her chest. She recognized the familiar feeling of fear as it pervaded her spirit. She was afraid of becoming too involved in Micah's life, which meant that she'd be in danger of exposing herself and her past.

"Please don't say no," Micah said, sensing her reluctance.

"Everything happens in His time, Micah, and not ours." Daniela's tone was solemn. "What if I pray and Mark doesn't wake up right away? Can you deal with that?"

"Yes," Micah replied.

"All right then," Daniela said. "I'd be happy to join you in praying for Mark. Just tell me when and where to meet you."

"There is a catch," he said with a sheepish grin. "The hospital's in Charleston, South Carolina." He cleared his throat. "I was hoping you'd have some time on Saturday to take the trip out there with me."

"Charleston?" She glanced down and bit her lower lip thoughtfully. She wished he'd divulged that information earlier. Then with the slightest uncertainty she said, "I guess I'd better dress comfortably for the long drive, right?"

Micah let out a long breath as though he'd been holding it in until she spoke. "Thank you for agreeing to do this, Daniela," he said with an appreciative nod.

They stood up, and she led him back to his car.

"I'll call you to finalize our plans for Saturday."

"Okay," she said.

They fell into an awkward silence. Micah realized he was still holding on to her arm and let it go.

"Goodnight," he said and turned his head away.

"Goodnight." Blushing, Daniela turned and walked back to her apartment, anxiously wondering if Micah had heard the sudden pounding of her heart.

At 6:00 a.m., the sun was peeking through the horizon and Daniela was rummaging through her closet to find a suitable outfit to wear for her three and a half hour long journey to Charleston with Micah. She stilled her motions and took a deep breath to calm herself from the anticipation and trepidation of being in such close proximity with Micah for such a lengthy period of time. Daniela placed her hands behind her neck and groaned miserably. She was conflicted every time she was around him, wanting to know him more and also keeping him far away.

"Why did I agree to do this?" She shook her head as she picked out black, loose-fitting jeans and a gold cashmere sweater.

After examining herself in the mirror, she picked through her cottony afro and groaned helplessly as she tried to pat it down into place. Suddenly she turned away from the mirror. What was she doing? Micah wouldn't be able to see her anyway. And besides, even if he could, it wouldn't have made a difference since they were on friendly terms and nothing more. *And that's the way it would remain,* she thought resolutely.

Chapter 16

The drive to Charleston was relatively quiet. Micah said very little, and Daniela could see that his mind was distant, undoubtedly thinking about his brother and the unknown circumstances of his condition. Once they'd made it to Charleston, Daniela glanced about her and could immediately sense the historical significance of the city. They passed several wartime monumental sites along the way to the hospital, and as they passed through the downtown area she marveled at the antiquated horse-drawn carriages that shared the roads with the cars.

"This seems like a nice and tranquil place to live," she thought aloud.

"It does have its charm." Micah nodded.

When they made it to the hospital, Daniela noticed how Micah's face became drawn and how he took several deep breaths to even out his breathing. Her eyes were filled with empathy.

"Are you ready to go inside?" she asked softly.

"There's something I didn't tell you." He tipped his head down. "My family and I don't get along too well, and I'm not looking forward to this reunion right now."

"Just tell yourself that you're here for Mark."

❖❖❖

Micah turned toward the building and heard footsteps all around them as people passed them by. Signaling that he was ready, they walked inside and Micah felt more at ease to have Daniela beside him. They stopped at the front desk to check in and to ask for information, and then proceeded toward the elevators. As the elevator inched its way upward, he straightened his shoulder and gripped the handle of his cane. *Here goes nothing,* he thought. He could sense Daniela watching him and tried to smile.

"You okay?" she asked.

He nodded.

They got off the elevator and edged toward Mark's room. Micah stopped just before they reached the door and turned to her.

"I have to do this part alone," he said quietly. "Please wait here for me?"

"Of course," she said.

He gave her hand a quick squeeze before letting it go. He walked the remaining steps to Mark's room. He took a deep breath before pushing open the door.

As soon as he stepped inside the hospital room Micah knew that all eyes were pinned on him. The silence was deafening and the tension in the air was almost suffocating. He gripped his cane tighter to stop the slight shaking of his hands and felt a line of sweat trickle down his back. He turned his head back and forth, waiting for someone to say something. But no one said a word. He took a deep breath.

"How's Mark?" he asked aloud.

Someone cleared his throat. "His vital signs are strong." The voice belonged to Uncle Joseph. "It's good to see you, Micah."

"Speak for yourself, Joseph," someone barked. Micah recognized it as his father's voice. Its deep cadence had not changed much over the years. "Where has he been all this time? Where has he been since this whole ordeal began weeks ago?" His father drew closer, his words cutting the air like clippers. And before Micah knew it, he'd received a blow across his face that sent him tumbling back.

"Morris, no!" Micah heard his mother yell out.

He could hear muffled cries from the corners of the room as he steadied himself and brought his hand to his wounded cheek. "It's always good to be with you, Dad," Micah said, his voice drenched with sarcasm.

"This isn't the time or the place for this, Mo," Micah heard his uncle's strained voice as he addressed his brother. "Now, you've got to calm down."

"Why, Micah?"

He turned to the sound of his mother's voice, her tears softening his indignation.

"Where have you been all this time, and why has it taken you this long to be here?"

Micah bit back his lips and his nostrils flared as he tried to control his emotions. "And for what, Mom. So everyone could welcome me with open arms, like they are doing right now?"

"We don't need your sarcasm," one of his male cousins uttered.

"Why come now?" someone else asked from the corner of the room. "Why not stay away altogether?"

It belonged to Aunt Lucinda, his Uncle Joseph's wife.

Micah let out an exasperated breath. "I'm here now and that should count for something."

"Not for much," his father spat out.

Micah ignored the jab. "I didn't come here to fight," he muttered. "I brought a friend who'd like to see Mark and to pray with him. Are there any objections?"

"What right have you got to bring anyone here when you haven't bothered to come yourself?" Morris Lambert continued the verbal onslaught.

Micah didn't respond.

"A little prayer couldn't hurt." He couldn't place the voice that tried to assist him and turned in the direction of the speaker questioningly.

"It's Robin, your cousin, Micah," she said in a soft voice.

He nodded gratefully.

After a few minutes of waiting, Micah turned around and walked toward the door. He called to Daniela and motioned for her to come inside.

As soon as Daniela walked inside the room she felt the tenseness that Micah had warned her about. She greeted everyone, and some tried to smile politely while others avoided looking at her altogether.

She turned toward the hospital bed and viewed Mark. Slowly she walked up to him and bowed her head. Though she couldn't feel God's presence Daniela began to pray, her eyes closed and her brows furrowed in intensity. She could hear others praying softly with her, and it gave her added strength.

When she'd finished praying Daniela touched Mark's forehead, searching his face for any signs of life. She could see his resemblance to Micah, though Mark's features were softer and more delicate than his brother's. Then she stepped back and surveyed the environment which was still tense. Daniela forced a polite smile. In the midst of the silence Micah said a stiff goodbye and then he sought Daniela's hand and they left the room together.

Once they were inside the limo, Daniela left Micah alone to process what'd taken place at the hospital and to decide how to deal with it. She understood his mood and gave him his personal space while in her mind she was reliving her own strained relationship with her father.

"I'm sorry," he said finally. "I'm just so angry at how hypocritical they're being right now."

She didn't protest when he directed his driver to stop at one of the many local seafood restaurants in the area so they could grab a bite to eat before they headed back to Charlotte.

Once they sat down and had placed their orders, Daniela was glad to see that Micah was in a more relaxed mood.

"So what did you think about the dysfunction in my family?" Micah said after a while, issuing a half-smile.

"I think we all have it in some form or another," Daniela said with a slight shrug. "I don't remember the last time my father and I have gotten along."

"What about your mother? Do you get along with her?"

Daniela hugged her arms against her chest and glanced downward, toying with the cloth napkin on her lap. "She passed away six years ago," she said briskly.

She was grateful for the interruption when the waiter brought their lunch orders. She'd ordered a grilled shrimp salad, and Micah had ordered the shrimp scampi.

"It's still a sore subject for you, am I right?" Micah asked after they'd blessed the food and commenced eating.

Momentarily, she was always intrigued by his precision as he sought to identify where the contents of his food were on his plate. Micah then fixed his eating utensils and his glass of cranberry juice in specific places where he could remember them, which facilitated his eating. His neatness and execution belied his blind condition.

"Yes," Daniela said after a long pause. "I don't really like to talk about it very much."

"You can talk to me," he prompted gently.

"Maybe some other time," she said quietly.

He nodded his understanding and took a sip of his drink. "For a long time I didn't want to talk about my past, either. In fact, I wanted to drink my problems away. But it doesn't heal the pain or take away the hurt and anger. And after a while you come to realize that you have no choice but to deal with it."

"How do you handle your problems now?" she asked cautiously.

"You mean do I still drink?" he said wryly. "Let's just say it's still a real struggle every day. But I'm determined to beat it."

"You know that God will not let you be tempted beyond what you can bear."

He pursed his lips and sat back, folding his arms against his chest. "Well, I learned a long time ago that I have to fight my own battles," he said. "If God was with me He wouldn't have let me lose my eyesight and I wouldn't have started drinking in the first place."

Daniela watched the sequence of emotions playing on his face, ranging from pain to anger, and back to pain and she felt her heart soften with compassion for him.

"God is with you, Micah, even if you can't see Him. And He wants to help you."

He didn't reply and they fell into an awkward silence.

"You're probably thinking that I'm not a good Christian brother," he said ruefully. "Not the type you'd like to be around."

"No, Micah." She shook her head. "I'm thinking you've been hurt like I have and it's hard to let it go."

He seemed to relax after hearing her response and the smile had returned on his face. "Thanks," Micah said.

"What for?"

"For not being judge and jury," he said with a shrug, "For being here and supporting me. I hope to return the favor."

"Well, you can," she said sheepishly. "This Sunday I'll be preaching my first sermon and I could use a friendly face in the crowd."

Micah didn't reply, and she grew anxious when she noticed the tense expression on his face.

"I'm sorry, Micah," she faltered. "I didn't mean to put you on the spot."

"No," he shook his head, "I want to be there for you."

"Are you sure?" she asked with uncertainty.

Micah nodded firmly and displayed a smile that put her mind more at ease.

"All right," she said. "Thank you."

"Besides, I owe you," he said. "Look how you've been here to support me through this drama with my family."

Daniela looked at him empathetically. "So what happens now between you and your family?"

Micah wiped his mouth with his napkin and pushed his plate away. "It's their call." He shrugged. "But I have to take responsibility for the part I played in our battles."

As she listened to Micah, Daniela thought about her own battle with her father. Could they ever repair the rift between them? She wasn't sure, but she knew that she'd also played a role in their broken relationship.

When they'd finished eating they left the restaurant and headed back to the limo. The drive to Charlotte was relatively quiet as they mused over their past, each nursing invisible wounds from old afflictions.

❖ ❖ ❖

Micah pushed his tongue against his wounded cheek as he recollected the scene in the hospital between him and his father. He'd known that it was going to be intense but he hadn't banked on Morris Lambert's right hook. If he wasn't so upset, he would've found it comical that at the age of thirty-seven he was still receiving a beating from his father.

Micah lay on his bed and placed his hands behind his head, trying not to think about the bottle that he'd poured down the drain some days ago. He grabbed his phone and called Ace.

"What's up, man?" his friend said.

Micah inhaled and let out his breath slowly. "I could use a little prayer tonight if that's okay."

"That's more than okay with me. Let's do this."

As Ace prayed, the cloud seemed to lift from on top of Micah's head and he thanked his friend.

"That's what brothers do for each other, right?"

"No doubt," Micah said before hanging up the phone with Ace.

Micah tried to think of happier times with his dad and their favorite activity to do together, which was to play catch in the yard and to collect baseball cards. Mark had been the intellectual, wanting to play chess instead of standing at bat or catching a fly ball with him and Dad. But it ended with the painful memories of losing his sight, which changed things between them.

Micah stood up and proceeded to do some exercises. The more he focused on the muscle tension in his body, the less he was consumed by the thoughts of the past. He was breathing hard from his workout but managed to strut toward the bathroom to shower.

Feeling better, Micah dressed for bed and was set to put the day behind him, when his uncle called. He ambled toward his nightstand and scrambled for the phone.

"What's going on, Uncle Joseph?" he said, frowning. His uncle's calls had become his only means of knowing what was going on with Mark, and he was anxious to hear what his uncle had to say.

"I'm glad you took my advice and came to the hospital but I wish you would've given me a heads up instead of surprising everyone, including me," his uncle said. "Maybe then I could've hinted at your arrival and maybe things wouldn't have gotten as out of hand as they did."

Micah stood in front of his bedroom window while speaking into the phone. He sighed and rubbed his eyelids. "We both know that things would've escalated whether they knew I was coming or not."

Uncle Joseph didn't disagree with the statement. "Well, son, your mother wants to talk to you. She's hoping she'll run into you at the hospital again real soon." He groaned loudly. "Now listen, Micah. They don't know that we've stayed in touch all this time, and I don't want them to because they'll feel like I betrayed them, which in a way I did."

"I understand, Uncle Jo."

The older man broke into a soft chuckle. "You really gave everybody a scare; it was like they saw the living dead."

Micah smiled faintly as he leaned up against the windowsill.

"Regardless of what your parents or anybody else thinks," his uncle added, "you hold your head up. You've grown into a fine young man, and I'm proud of you, Micah."

"Thanks, Uncle Jo," he said gruffly.

Chapter 17

Daniela walked up and down the living room floor, reading her sermon aloud. She suddenly stopped and marveled at the greatness of God. As it turned out, the trip to Charleston with Micah proved to be what God had in mind. She'd come home and immediately went right to work making the necessary revisions to give the sermon more depth. The scene at the hospital had made her see that in a family, relationships can be destroyed when the members don't reach out to one another and to forgive each other, but rather remained in a state of bitterness.

She cleared her throat and began to read aloud from her written pages. "The glue that is needed to hold the family together is found in Christ. Only He can come into the situation and through the power of the Holy Spirit, heal the wounds and remove the bitterness. And as the family of God, the church must forgo bitterness and strife among them and come together to advance the cause of Christ, and to spread His gospel message in word and in deed so that it can be an effective witness to others."

Smiling, Daniela sat down and put the final touches to her sermon and then she thought about Micah and his family, hoping that God would bring them healing so that they can be a family once again. Then she was convicted to pray for her own relationship with her father, but she knew that it would take more time and effort on her part to do what God was asking her to do, which was to forgive her father.

Sunday morning came much too soon for Daniela. She was jumpy as she went about the task of getting ready for church. No amount of tea could settle the queasiness of her stomach. She took deep breaths and went over the introduction to the sermon in her mind, and then she made sure she packed up the sermon outline so that she wouldn't forget it.

Daniela forced down a light breakfast, all the while glancing at the clock. She rushed to give herself another glance over. This morning she decided to apply more eye-shadow and blush than usual on top of her natural-based foundation. She peered at her suit—a brown and white ensemble that she'd topped with a green broach that her grandmother had given her—and took a deep breath before dashing out of the room and out the door.

She was en route to pick up Micah, which she'd promised to do, and sped up slightly to try and beat the clock. Thankfully, his apartment complex was not far from hers, though theirs were worlds apart in exclusivity and accommodations. His complex was inside a gated community; she had to get his permission to enter into it. As she circled around a wide curb which led to the apartment buildings, Daniela glimpsed the massive and luxurious properties, with their manicured lawns, sculpted hedges, and grand water fountains.

When she got to his building Micah was already standing outside waiting for her. He looked handsome in a brownish striped suit, white shirt, and burgundy tie.

"You look very nice," she said as she approached him.

"I imagine you do too."

They stood silently, each waiting for the other to speak.

"We should get going," she said finally. "May I direct you to the car?"

She guided him to the passenger side of the car and he slipped inside. She took her seat behind the wheel and pulled the car around the wide curb of the front entrance, retraced her path back to the security gate, and exited the complex. They drove in silence for a short while and Daniela surveyed Micah again. He was bouncing his foot up and down in a nervous motion.

"I like your apartment complex," she said. "It's very luxurious."

"Thanks." His face was aimed at the passenger side window.

"Have you lived there long?"

"The past three years."

She frowned at his curt replies. *Maybe he's having a bad morning,* she thought. She stopped trying to make conversation. Instead Daniela focused on the road and recited the introduction to her sermon in her mind. She tried not to pay any attention to the queasiness in her stomach or the dryness in her throat, but the closer she got to the church the more nervous she became.

"I'll be honest with you, Daniela." Micah cut into her train of thought. "I haven't been to church in years.

Apart from work related activity I keep dealings with people to a minimum. When you're like me you become a freak of nature to many." He shook his head dejectedly. "I'm doing this because I want to be there for you."

She glanced over at him with a sad look on her face. "I'm sorry, Micah. I didn't consider how difficult this might be for you," she said. "If you want I can take you back home."

"No," he mouthed. "I won't let you do that."

With a heavy conscience, Daniela pulled into the crowded parking lot of Bethel Baptist Church. It was a brown brick steeple building that was modest in size. But everything else about the church was grand, including the Spirit-led and Spirit-filled worship. Daniela had felt completely at home the moment she'd stepped inside the doors of Bethel after searching for a church home during her initial move to Charlotte.

Now she parked as close to the building as she could and glanced anxiously in Micah's direction. "Are you sure you're okay with attending the service?"

"Don't worry, I'll be fine." He tried to smile, but she could see beads of sweat forming along his brow. "I'd like you to focus on what you're here to do."

She stepped out of the car and walked around to Micah's side, hovering close by as he exited the car. "I'll make sure that you get the best seat possible so that no one will bother you," she said.

He raised her hand to his lips and kissed it. "I trust you."

Daniela blushed as she led him through the parking lot, along the way greeting some members and ignoring their looks of curiosity. One of them was Sister Jackie, a woman that Daniela had connected with right away when she became a member of Bethel. She was walking along the path toward the front entrance with her husband and teenage son.

"There are a few steps to climb," Daniela whispered to Micah once they'd reached the side entrance of the church. Patiently, she pointed out each step and waited for him to mount each one and then they crossed the threshold into the sanctuary. Daniela's heart began to beat speedily against her chest. She glanced around and saw that some parishioners were already seated.

She walked Micah to the front pew and sat him down there so that he wouldn't be trampled on by people's feet or be brushed up against by strangers as they sought to jump over him to sit down. She then alerted the ushers and told them that he was her guest so that they would not bother him.

"I'll be heading to the back now to speak with my pastor and to prepare," she whispered to him. "Can I get you anything before I go?"

He shook his head smiling. "I know you'll do well up there."

"Thank you." She patted his hand before walking off.

Daniela paced back and forth inside Pastor Sanders' office, which he'd given her permission to use as she prepped to speak. Fully alert, she listened to the praise and worship portion of service and then the announcements, waiting for her turn to come. When it arrived, she stepped out into the hall and walked toward the stage entrance. It was as though she were treading shaky ground.

With Pastor Sanders' introduction, Daniela walked out onto the podium and stood in front of the pulpit.

She could hear her heart beating one hundred or more beats per minute. She took deep breaths and stole a glance at Micah. He looked out of sorts, as he held on to his cane like an anchor. But he also looked determined as though he were dead set on finishing a task he'd started.

Daniela said a prayer to dispel the nervous tension she felt, and immediately felt calmed.

"We all know what it's like to be in a family where there is strife and division." She looked around the sanctuary, feeling more confident with every word. "And where there's division, the family will fall apart.

"The same is true for believers in Christ. We belong to God's family and we must seek to be united with one another and not be divided. Only then can we make a difference in this world and win souls for Christ." She gripped the podium, her voice now ringing with emotion. "In John 13:35, our Lord Jesus spoke with His disciples and told them that everyone will know they are His disciples if they love one another.

"As modern day disciples of our Lord, we need to display that same love for each other so that we can be effective witnesses to the world about who we serve."

Daniela heard some scattered "amens" and saw some heads bobbing to the message. She also saw some looks of disapproval being shot in her direction. One of them belonged to the young preacher, Mason Goodwin who was in the audience.

She didn't stop to ponder their looks, but kept pushing ahead with the message, gathering strength from those responding to the Word.

"Let's put God's agenda before our own," she concluded, "and to seek to be united in body and in spirit as Christ commanded of us."

Once she'd left the pulpit and retreated back to Pastor Sanders' office, Daniela's knees buckled to the ground and she prayed to God with thanksgiving in her heart.

Pastor Sanders came to her and beamed. "God bless you, Sister Daniela," he said. "God used you in a mighty way this morning."

She thanked him and willingly followed suit as he stood beside the church exit door to greet the congregation as they left the church premises. While on her way to meeting with Micah, Daniela was detained by several other members who sought to shake her hand. She tried to keep the conversations brief in consideration of Micah who sat patiently waiting for her.

"How are you?" she asked him when she finally reached him.

Pressing his lips together firmly, he gave a short nod of approval. "I heard the conviction in your voice, and it rang with emotion and authority. You should be proud, Daniela."

"I thank God; He did all the work, I just stood there."

"Well, it takes guts to just stand there and be used."

"Thank you," she said appreciatively. "Are you ready to go?"

Micah nodded and stood. Before they could walk out, Daniela heard her name being called. She turned around to see Pastor Goodwin coming towards her. Planting a smile on her face, she greeted him and then she introduced him to Micah.

"I'd like us to get together sometime and talk about why the Lord has allowed our paths to cross," Pastor Goodwin said to Daniela.

"Yes, that would be fine."

"I look forward to spending time with a beautiful woman of God."

His comment made Daniela blush and she heard Micah take a harried breath.

"Well, I won't keep you much longer. Let's set up something real soon." He glanced at Micah and then at Daniela. "Have a good afternoon."

"Good afternoon, Pastor Goodwin," she responded thinly.

Daniela pulled out of the parking lot and felt a surge of energy after what'd transpired in church. She could barely contain her joy after preaching to the congregation for the first time. She replayed the moments in her mind and fought feebly against a smile that'd spread across her face. She didn't notice Micah's brooding silence nor did she see his terse expression as he angled his face toward the passenger side window.

"Thank you for coming, Micah, and for supporting me," she said, while merging into traffic. "I appreciate it, especially now that I know it wasn't easy for you to do."

He didn't respond at first. Then carefully, he asked, "Who is Pastor Goodwin?"

Daniela glanced in Micah's direction questioningly. "I don't really know him. He's visited our church a few times and I talked to him once before."

Micah turned in her direction. "He acts like he knows *you* pretty well."

"What do you mean?"

"It's obvious he's interested in you."

She set her jaw tightly, her former joy quickly fading. "Even if that were the case, I'm not interested in him."

"Does he know that?"

Daniela sighed exasperatedly. "I don't understand why we're talking about this."

"You're right. Let's just forget about it."

The sound of Christian contemporary music tunes were playing on the car radio and interjected their moody silence. Neither of them spoke again until they neared Micah's apartment complex.

Bending her head slightly, Daniela tried to shrug off her anger as she felt reminded of the unifying message she'd just preached a little while earlier. She summoned the strength to glance over at Micah, and apologized to him as she came to a full stop in front of his building's entrance.

Micah gripped the car door handle, but didn't motion to exit the car. He appeared to be searching for the right words to express how he felt about her.

"I'm sorry too, Daniela," he said quietly. "But this is where you and I are very different. I'm willing to look beyond the surface to see what lies underneath." He paused. "And what I see with us is . . . something deeper . . . something I'm willing to explore if you're willing to take the journey with me."

She hung her head and sighed, wondering how to respond to Micah's disclosure. "I thought we agreed to be friends," she said, her voice sounding uncertain.

"Friends are honest with each other, Daniela." His tone was delicate but pointed. "Tell me you don't feel that there's something more between us. If you don't want to be honest with me, at least be honest with yourself."

After a long, tense pause Micah stepped out of the car and made his way inside his apartment building. Daniela gazed after him momentarily, her heart squeezing tightly against her chest, its gush of feelings barricaded by fear.

Micah sat at the kitchen table and shoved a mouthful of rice and peas inside his mouth, chewing sullenly. Though the restaurant-bought meal was finely seasoned, Micah's mood proportioned it to dirt. He stood up to put the plate in the sink, but his motion was too quick and he banged his thighs against the edge of the table. Frustrated, he grumbled, pushed the plate away, and got up from the table.

Micah ambled toward the brown sectional leather sofa in the living room and plopped down on it. He was angry with Daniela for choosing to ignore what was happening between them; he was especially mad at himself for giving another woman the power to break his heart.

He leaned back against the couch and rubbed his face with his hands. "Why did she come into my life if she wasn't the one for me?" Micah asked aloud. "I don't get it."

His phone rang; it was Uncle Joseph. He answered and was happy to receive his uncle's report about Mark's improved condition.

"At least I have some good news to brighten my day," he said.

"What's the matter, son?"

Why not tell him about my love woes? Micah resigned. Uncle Joseph was a wise man who'd always given him good advice in the past. After only a moment's hesitation Micah decided to confide in his uncle about Daniela.

"I met this woman and I think we can have something really special, but I can't seem to get through to her."

"What's the problem?"

"I don't know, Uncle Jo." Micah leaned forward resting his elbows above his knees and gesturing with his free hand. "She and I seem to hit it off. But she keeps her guard up pretty tight. I can't seem to penetrate."

"Does she know how you feel about her?"

Micah suppressed a groan as he thought about his jealous rant earlier when he and Daniela were coming back from church. "Let's just say she's getting the picture."

With a sobering tone Uncle Joseph asked, "Do you think her hesitation has something to do with your being blind, son?"

"The thought has crossed my mind," Micah admitted. He leaned back against the couch. "But she's not shallow, Uncle Jo." Micah searched for the words to explain how connected he felt to Daniela. "You see, she understands what it's like to have people judge you on the outside, and she's dead set against doing that to others. So I have to think that there's more to her resistance than that."

"You need to stop guessing and ask her what the problem is."

"But that might push her away even more."

"Maybe," his uncle said. "But then again maybe you're not pushing hard enough."

"What do you mean?"

"Maybe she needs someone to show that they care enough about her to find out what's wrong. Probe deeper and you may discover what the problem is and in the process win the young lady's heart with your care and concern."

"Probe deeper, huh?" Micah thought about what his uncle said and acknowledged the wisdom behind his words. Perhaps she was placed in his life for him to help her fix whatever problem she was dealing with. But Micah couldn't help but to wonder if that was going to cost him what was left of his heart.

After Daniela got home from church she did her best to forget about the disagreement she'd had with Micah. She tried watching television but nothing seemed to hold any interest for her. Then she went into cleaning mode, which always seemed to have a calming effect on her. She started out in the kitchen and then worked her way to the rest of the apartment until everything was shiny and spotless.

But after a while the thoughts crept into her mind anyway, and soon she was reliving those tense moments inside the car. It always ended with Micah saying that she wasn't being honest with herself. Daniela sighed as she paced about the living room in deep reflection. If she were being honest, she'd have to admit that she did want a meaningful relationship with Micah. But her fears told her that she wasn't ready for this level of commitment, even though there was no doubt in her mind that he was. The thought made her anxious because she didn't know how to make him see that his pursuit of her was pointless. She didn't want to hurt him because she had become an island unto herself.

Chapter 18

Daniela woke up determined to forget her troubles and concentrate on the food and clothing she was taking to the church later that morning. Grateful that the weather had warmed up a bit, she was hoping for a good turnout. So many people needed the provisions that they were trying to collect. Each time she considered how over twelve-thousand people in North Carolina alone were homeless she shuttered.

"It shouldn't be this way," she said aloud and shook her head regretfully as she taped up a box full of non-perishable items.

Her cell phone rang and for a split second her heart banged against her chest with a thud as thoughts of Micah came to mind. Shamefully, she'd been dodging his calls. Now she stole a peek at the caller ID and exhaled the breath she was holding when she realized the caller was Sister Jackie.

"Hey, Sister Jackie."

"How are you, Sister Daniela?" Her tone was deep and boisterous as she gave Daniela a quick update on the morning activities. "I wanted you to know that we're here and we're getting the tables set up. You'll also be glad to know that people are starting to show up with their donations already."

"That's great. Can you please make sure that we have enough Thank you pins and buttons to give out to the people who make donations? I should be at the church shortly."

"Yes, ma'am. I'll take care of the pins and I'll see you soon."

After hanging up the phone Daniela placed her hands on her hips and glanced down at the boxes she'd just finished putting together with mild consternation, suddenly wishing that she occupied a main level apartment or at least a building with an elevator, since having neither meant having to lug those boxes down the stairs. Without further delay, she heaved the first box of goods down the cemented steps and nearly lost her footing as she attempted to haul it inside the trunk of her car. Her eyes fell on the donations Micah had given, which were already neatly stored away inside the trunk and her heart pulsated with emotion.

After placing the additional boxes in the backseat of the car, Daniela got behind the wheel and mechanically drove into traffic as thoughts of Micah continued to assail her. She felt guilty about avoiding his phone calls but she knew this was the way things had to be. She had to stop whatever it was that was happening between them before things went too far. Or maybe they already had. Daniela sighed and shook her head vigorously for a second, trying to focus on the task at hand. She needed to stop thinking about what could never be and, instead, focus on the one thing in her life that she could count on to bring her joy and fulfillment and that was doing the Lord's work.

Before stopping at the deli shop to pick up breakfast for her ministry crew, Daniela swung by a toy store to retrieve toys for the needy children. She wanted to make sure that in the midst of helping the adults, the kids' needs weren't being neglected. It bothered her to consider that there were kids out there whose hunger pangs kept them from enjoying their childhood, which involved playing with toys. She purchased as many toys as she could afford, ranging from trucks and little robots to Barbie dolls and stuffed animals. She smiled sadly as she rubbed the head of a stuffed teddy bear and recalled her own childhood, which had been cut short by the horrors that life could bring. She hoped that this little teddy bear would show a child that good things still happened in this life, by the grace of God. But as she thought about that she couldn't deny God's Spirit questioning if she believed what she preached.

Micah took the long drive to Charleston alone this time. When he arrived at the hospital to visit his brother, Micah had to remind himself that he wasn't in control of the situation. He forced himself to put one foot in front of the other as he made his way up to his brother's room. Still, he was aware of something that he was missing, which was making the trip even more weighty, and that was Daniela. Her presence had brought him comfort and had been a welcoming source of support for him. It was disheartening that she wasn't with him now. But Micah pushed those thoughts aside as the elevator doors swung open. He popped his head up and stepped out into the hall. Right now he needed to gather all his strength to contend with the emotional stand-offs with his family.

Micah made his way through the hall and counted the short distance it took to get to Mark's room. He took a deep breath and braced himself for another verbal, and perhaps physical, confrontation with his family before opening the door. But there was no stirring inside and no echo of sounds.

"Is anyone here?"

When he received no response Micah breathed out and his shoulder muscles relaxed. He turned his head in the direction of Mark's hospital bed and slowly walked a short distance until his cane made contact with the metal frame of the bedpost. A feeling of woe washed over him as he stood alone with his brother for the first time. He searched his brain for something meaningful to say; something that would make Mark hear him and wake up.

"Do you remember how we used to run off on exploratory ventures on the estate in the summertime and on weekends?" Micah let out a short laugh. "We'd carry compasses and go looking for gold like we were Columbus or Marco Polo or something.

"You and I had some good times together when we weren't fighting or competing for our parents' attention," he added quietly.

Micah reached out and touched the edge of the bed and searched around for his brother's hand. When he'd found it, he held on and squeezed. "You need to wake up now, Mark," he said. His words were caught in his throat as he fought to control his grief. "We need you," he whispered.

Micah turned around when he heard someone enter the room.

"I'm glad you're here, Micah." It was his mother.

He didn't reply, turning back toward Mark.

She approached him slowly and stood close by but didn't reach out to touch him.

"Where's everyone else?" he asked.

"We take turns keeping vigil. No one else is here right now but me."

They stood silently, and Micah still held on to his brother's hand.

"I never stopped praying that you would find your way back to us," she said softly.

"Too bad it had to be under these circumstances," he responded in a dry tone.

"We have to talk this out, my son," Ann Lee Lambert said quietly. "Regardless of what you think of us, we're still your family."

"It's what you all think of me that's the problem, Mom."

She gasped slightly, as though he'd struck her. "You have it all wrong."

"I don't agree," he said calmly. Micah gently set down Mark's hand and turned away. "I have to go, Mom."

"Wait, Micah, please." She wanted to reach out to him but her hand stalled in midair. "At least tell me when you'll be back here again. We can't leave things as they are. For Mark's sake we need to try and make amends." Her tone was stressed, like a chord that was stretched too thin and was on the verge of breaking. "Or do you think running is still the answer for everything?"

Micah's back stiffened. "I'm here, aren't I?"

"Then be present all the time, Micah," she said in an even tone. "Let's come back together as a family and be here for Mark together. He needs all of us now."

"And our falling out is all my fault, right Mom?"

"I'm not saying it is. But I am saying that you're not making it any easier each time you walk away from us."

"I want to be here, but I don't want to have to fight you all to be here, either."

He heard his mother's audible sigh. "The only one you're fighting is yourself, Micah."

"What is that supposed to mean?"

"When you accept yourself for who you are, my son, it doesn't matter who else accepts you." She reached for him this time, gripping his hand. Micah winced but didn't pull his hand away. "There's no more excuses, Micah. Either you show up or you don't. The decision is yours and no one else's."

"I'll be here," he said gruffly.

"Good," his mom replied.

Micah left the hospital with his mother's words digging into the rough patches of his heart like pointy daggers of truth. He shrank from them because he didn't want to face the reality of his past and present choices, which had and would determine what happened next.

Chapter 19

When Daniela failed to call Micah back, he decided to give Claudia's proposition some consideration. Micah blocked out the voice in his head that signaled making the wrong choice and welcomed the careless freedom of operating without reserve.

Presently, he and Claudia were having dinner together at an upscale Chinese restaurant they used to frequent when they were still together. As Micah waited for Claudia to emerge from the powder room, he tried to recall the good times they'd had together, and to convince himself that he was right where he wanted to be. Micah took a sip of his cranberry juice. He stood up briefly when Claudia returned to the table.

"I'm sorry to keep you waiting, sugar," Claudia said as she was helped to her seat by a waiter. She reached for Micah's hand. "It feels like old times being back here with you, Micah."

Micah pressed his lips together into a tight smile. "I remember this used to be your favorite restaurant."

"It still is."

"Fill me in on a few things," he said casually, as he withdrew his hand from hers. "What's been going on with you since we parted ways?"

"You mean apart from missing you?" she said playfully.

"Right." He played along. "Apart from that."

"Why rehash the past?" she said with a pout. "Let's focus on starting a future . . . together."

"Humor me." Micah felt for his glass, which he'd placed strategically to his right, and took another sip of cranberry juice.

"Well, if you must know, I've kept busy with work." She shrugged. "An attorney's work is never done."

"You've always been ambitious, Claudia, and especially with your move into politics."

"If I recall correctly, sugar, you were just as hungry as I was."

"Then things changed, didn't they."

"Come on," she said, tugging at his arm playfully. "Let's talk about you and me right now."

"Okay," he said willingly. "Has there been anyone else since we broke up?"

They were interrupted by the waiter who brought their food to the table. After the waiter left, he prompted her to answer his question.

"That's easy," she said. "No, there hasn't."

Micah twisted his mouth sideways as though unconvinced. He felt around for his cloth napkin and placed it on his lap. He then gripped his fork to bite into his broccoli beef with fried rice but stopped abruptly. "Do you mind if we say grace?"

"When did you get all religious?" she asked curiously.

He thought about Daniela and tipped his head downward. "I was reminded of its importance by a friend. You mind?"

"No, I guess not," she said.

After he'd prayed over the food, Micah took a careful bite of his fried rice and then he set down his fork and wiped his mouth.

"When we were together you were the one who wanted to get married, while I wanted to wait till we were ready." He spoke with a hint of amusement in his voice. "Do you still want that? And how about having kids? Can you work that into your busy schedule, or will it interfere with your political ambitions?"

Claudia coughed on the sweet and sour chicken she was eating and took a drink of her water. Micah couldn't help but to chuckle.

"Very funny, Mr. Lambert," she said with mock seriousness. "If you're proposing, I say there'll be plenty of time for babies, and let's just work on the engagement and the wedding first."

Micah took another bite of his food and chewed thoughtfully. "A smart man doesn't make hasty decisions. And I don't want to discount the possibility that there can be something between us again, Claudia. But to be honest with you I have strong feelings for someone else."

"Oh, so you finally admit that there is someone else," Claudia mused. "You're just a little bit confused right now, sugar. But that'll change once you and I are back on track."

"You've always been sure of yourself, Claudia," Micah said, smiling. "That's one of the things I always admired about you."

"One among many other things, right?" Claudia said. He heard her throaty laugh and felt her hand caress his arm. "I say we take the rest of this meal to go and you can tell me all about the many other qualities you like about me."

Micah tried to swallow the sudden lump in his throat. "I want to say yes, Claudia, and that's a dangerous place to be."

"Come on." She purred. "It'll be fun."

"I'm sure it will be," he said with a wry smile. "We never had trouble having fun. It was everything else that we couldn't get right."

"But it'll be different this time," she insisted.

After Micah paid for their meal and they stood up to leave, Claudia clung to his arm. "So what do you say, your place or mine?"

As they sat down together inside his limo, Micah felt the pressure of Claudia's body against his own. It reminded him of liquor, and how he was tempted to drink each time he was around it. Like alcohol, he had to fight hard to resist Claudia or else he'd live to regret it the next day.

Micah moved over in his seat, placing a sizeable distance between them. He directed his driver to take Ms. Beauchamp home, and then to take him to his own place.

Claudia clucked her tongue disappointedly. "You never could say no to me for very long, you know. I'll wear you down yet," she added with a pout.

"Yeah," he said. "That's what I'm afraid of."

Chapter 20

Micah's mouth practically dropped to the floor when he heard the news. "You're not kidding me, are you, Uncle Jo?" he finally uttered.

"I wouldn't do that to you, son, not over something this serious," Joseph said barely containing his contentment. "Mark's awake, Micah. The doctors are checking him out as we speak to see if there're any permanent damages from the assault, but I can tell you right away that he's fine. It's a miracle."

"Indeed it is," Micah said distantly. "Does he remember what happened to him?" he asked.

"We haven't had a chance to really talk to him yet. But you'll have to make another trip down to the hospital to find out for yourself. I'm sure he'll want to see all of his family, and that includes you."

Micah's excitement waned as he considered what a reunion with his brother would be like. He wasn't certain about how Mark was going to receive him. "I'm not so sure about that, Uncle Jo, but I'll be there anyway."

After speaking with his uncle, Micah knew he had to reach Daniela to tell her the good news about Mark's recovery. She'd been there for him, praying for Mark when he asked for her help. So she had every right to know that her prayers had not been in vain. Now acquainted with her schedule, Micah knew that she'd be home so he had his driver take him to her apartment. Since she'd been avoiding his calls, he decided on another tactic. Instead of calling her, he texted her using the Braille keypads from his cell phone. Micah stepped out of the vehicle which was parked at the curb near her apartment building and waited anxiously for her to respond.

Daniela read and reread the text message that was flashing across the screen of her cell phone:

PLEASE MEET ME DOWNSTAIRS.

I HAVE SOME NEWS TO SHARE WITH YOU.

She jumped up and raced to the window, easily spotting Micah's limo with him leaning against it. Her heartbeats seemed to stumble over one another as she considered what to do next. What did he want to tell her, and more importantly was she prepared to hear it? After pacing about the floor of the living room for a few minutes, she grabbed her jacket and keys.

As she drew closer to Micah, she was surprised by the sudden dancing of her spirit in reaction to seeing him. She realized that she'd missed him.

"I'm here," she said hoarsely.

He pushed away from the car and took a few steps forward. Micah could only pray that his voice was steady as he uttered, "I'm glad you are."

Daniela broke the silence that ensued. "You had some news you wanted to share?"

He nodded. "Mark's awake, Daniela."

"That's great, Micah," she said excitedly. Forgetting her reserve for the moment, she crossed the distance between them and clasped his hand. "God is faithful."

"He is." Micah smiled and squeezed her hand in return. "I was hoping you'd go to the hospital again with me to see him."

She slipped her hand from his grasp. "I'd like to, Micah. But I don't think I can."

He sighed. "Listen, Daniela. To be honest I'd love to have you there with me for some moral support," he said soberly. "But I respect your decision not to go."

Anxiously, Daniela watched him turn away, and she felt heaviness invade her heart. She knew he needed a friend right now, and she couldn't ignore his plea. "Wait, Micah," she said. "I'll go with you."

He turned back toward her and smiled, his expression melting away the residual doubts in her heart. "Thank you."

Hours later Micah and Daniela stood together in silence as the hospital elevator inched its way up to the eighth floor. Micah could barely mask his conflicted feelings— on the one hand he was elated to know that Mark was awake, but on the other hand, he was uneasy about the reunion with his brother.

"Mark made it, Micah," Daniela told him as they stepped out of the elevator. "God healed him completely. There's no reason to be fearful anymore."

He sighed. "You don't know the whole story, Daniela. But I'll fill you in later," he muttered.

He held on to the bend of her elbow and also tapped his cane along the linoleum floor of the hospital as they made their way to Mark's room.

Micah stopped in front of the door and took a deep breath before he signaled for them to go inside. But soon they discovered that no one was there.

"Maybe they moved him to another room or another floor," Daniela offered as they stepped back out to the hall. "Wait here and I'll go ask someone at the nurses' station."

Micah nodded. As an orderly moved a bedded patient through the halls, Micah backed away and bumped someone from behind. "I'm sorry," he said.

"It's me, Cousin Micah. I can take you to Cousin Mark. They moved him to another room on the same floor."

"Robin?"

"Yes," she said, smiling.

He tilted his head upward slightly. "Thanks, little cousin. You seem to always come to my rescue." Micah smiled. "Listen, I have a friend with me. She should be back any second and then you can take us both to see Mark, okay?"

"Sure," she said.

"How is Mark doing?" Micah asked.

"He's getting antsy about leaving the hospital already. He's telling everybody that he's fine and he's ready to go home."

"One of the nurses confirmed that they moved him to another room," Daniela said as she walked up to them, "since his condition has improved."

Micah turned toward her and nodded. "My little cousin here has already filled me in." Micah made the introductions and soon they were walking toward Mark's room together.

When they approached Mark's door, Robin whispered, "We're here."

Micah slid his hand down from Daniela's arm to her hand and held it. He took a deep breath and they followed Robin inside the room. Just as before, the murmurs quieted down, and there was a nervous tension in the room as thick as smog. But this time there was the added suspense of knowing that Mark was awake and looking straight at him.

Micah felt Daniela's hand tighten around his and lamented bringing her into his family feud. He wondered what she was seeing. Undoubtedly, she was looking about her at stern and bewildered faces, and hoping to find a friendly one in the crowd.

"Are you okay?" she whispered to him.

Micah nodded though he felt like he was on the verge of breaking down.

"Mark?" he called out. He wanted so badly to gaze upon his brother and to see that he was all right for himself. "Hello, Mark," he called out.

He didn't get a response, and Micah wondered if he'd been heard.

"I don't know whether to hug you or to lug you," a distant voice suddenly echoed from the left side of the room. "So I'll do neither."

The slight trembling of Micah's chin disclosed his turbid emotions and he cleared his throat and swallowed down the lump that was lodged there.

"Either way I'm glad you're awake," he said. "How do you feel?"

"I'm still breathing."

"Do you need anything?"

"I think you've done enough," his father's harsh rebuff rang out. "You can't just stroll in here and pretend like you've been a part of his life all this time."

"That's not what I'm trying to do," Micah said quietly. After a long stretch of silence, he sighed and turned around to leave.

"Don't go, Micah," his mother entreated. "Come and sit down."

He stopped but did not turn around. "I'll leave that up to Mark. Do you want me to stick around, Mark?"

When his brother didn't respond Micah took that as affirmation that his presence was not wanted. He pulled Daniela alongside him as he edged toward the door and out into the hall. They moved across the quiet halls of the hospital floor and to the elevators without speaking.

Chapter 21

"Do you want to talk about it?" Daniela finally asked as they sat inside the limo headed back to Charlotte.

He wanted her to know his struggles and he wanted to know hers and that began with self-disclosure. If Micah wanted Daniela to trust him, he would have to set the tone by entrusting her with his life's story.

He turned his head toward the passenger side window of the car as if he were watching a movie reel and he relayed to her what he was seeing in the deep recesses of his mind. The images were distant but their wounds so fresh, they seemed to have happened yesterday.

Micah was an angry young man when he left home. Unwilling to turn back but unsure of how to move forward, Micah stayed boarded up in his Uncle Joseph's guestroom, a blind 20-year-old with an attitude and no hope for the future. One day his uncle confronted him.

"You know you can stay here as long as you want, Micah. But you got to get yourself together, son. Life is not going to stop just because you up here feeling sorry for yourself."

"What can I do, Uncle Jo? How can I accomplish anything when I can't even see my hands in front of my face?" he said testily.

His uncle walked over to the bed where he lay and sat at the edge of it. "You can start by making the most of what you do have. You're smart and very resourceful. You can do great things if you set your mind to it."

"If you don't mind, I'd like to be alone." Though he knew his uncle meant well, the last thing he wanted to hear was a pep talk.

"Well I do mind." His uncle stood up abruptly. "I think it's time for prayer, son."

"You know I don't believe in that stuff anymore." Anger seeped into his voice. "What kind of God would allow someone to lose his sight just like that and ruin their life like He did?"

"A good and a mighty God, Micah," Joseph said soberly. "Even when we go through things that we don't understand; this doesn't have to be the end of your life, but could be the beginning of another life for you. Something you never would've thought or dreamed of."

Micah turned his head away, wishing he could walk away from the entire conversation.

"Humor me, son." Uncle Jo gripped his shoulder and then he prayed for God to reveal a plan and a purpose for Micah's life; to give him a vision that even he would've never consider for himself.

Micah took a deep breath before divulging the second half of his story. It was easier to recount the triumphs of continuing his education at a school for the blind where he was prepared for employment and entrepreneurship and also for how to become adept at independent living. The hard part was relaying how the years of feeling betrayed by his family contributed to some poor choices he made, like taking up drinking to dull the pain, something he thought he would never do.

"Thankfully, it never got to the point where I was passing out or hugging the toilet bowl," Micah said with a smirk. "But when the drinking started to cloud my judgment and put my business in jeopardy, I made a vow to never drink again. But that's been harder to do than I thought."

"You've been through a lot, Micah." Daniela touched his hand and gave it a supportive squeeze. "But I hope you realize just how blessed you are."

He didn't speak right away, turning his head toward the sound of a train in the distance. "For so long I felt like I'd been gypped. The blessings I should've received went to someone else and I was left in the dust." Micah shook his head, gritting his teeth as he spoke. "I was so angry with God, telling Him that He was unfair. And that while He was dolling out blessings to everyone else, why couldn't He bless even me? But He doesn't always bless us how we want Him to, does He?"

"No," Daniela said, smiling. "No, He doesn't."

"I used to wonder why God didn't just take me instead of make me blind and useless.

"I couldn't shake the feeling that I wasn't good enough for them." Micah blew air out of his mouth to control his emotions. "When I left, I said I'd never look back. That I didn't need them because I could make it on my own."

Micah leaned back against his seat feeling deflated. "Now all I want is their love and acceptance."

"I know the feeling." Daniela said. "It's like you spend your whole life trying to prove them wrong, only to find out that being right isn't all that important anymore."

"And that being right can be the loneliest feeling in the world," he added with a rueful smile.

"Right," she added.

"You know my story." Micah turned toward her. "Now it's your turn."

"I left home because I needed to leave behind the pain of the things that happened to my family, or I would never move past it. But now I'm learning that sometimes it takes more than time and distance to heal old wounds," she said.

"Does this pain have anything to do with your mother?"

"Yes. After she died, I moved to Charlotte to leave the past behind. But it's hard to run from something that is always with you."

"What are you running from?" Micah asked gently.

She sighed. "A past I don't want to repeat."

"You're not giving me much to go on," he said with a half-smile.

"I'm sorry," she said. "It's still hard for me to talk about."

He nodded, understanding. "It's all right. When you're ready to talk I'll be here." He cocked his head to the side and leaned closer, her jasmine scented perfume filling his nostrils. "In the meantime, do you think you'll ever retire those running shoes? I'll give up mine if you'll give up yours."

Daniela laughed. "That's a tall order since they've been broken in and are very comfortable."

"Yeah, like my funky and torn pair." Micah joined in her laughter and soon after they fell into a comfortable silence.

"I've missed our talks." His face was hidden and his voice was above a whisper. "I thought we were really connecting and I miss that. I was hoping you did too."

"I do," she said. "But I don't want to confuse things between us."

"I'm not confused, Daniela. I know that you and I have something special happening between us, and I believe it's something God is putting together." He turned in her direction, imagining the anxious expression on her face. "What I don't get is why you won't let it happen."

She didn't respond.

"I thought you were a woman of faith, Daniela."

"Scripture says to put our faith in God and not in man, Micah," Daniela retorted defensively. "When you put your faith in man all you're left with is a broken heart."

The limo pulled up along the curb next to her apartment building.

Micah's tone was sad and his expression sober giving Daniela pause, as he stated, "Is it fair to make someone pay for someone else's mistake?"

"I have to go," she said hoarsely. He heard her exit the limo and the sound of her shoes as she raced toward her apartment.

For days she couldn't get his words out of her mind. Micah's vision of what they could be to each other mesmerized her like a wonderful fantasy. Daniela tortured herself with such a possibility, though she knew that it could never happen until she'd dealt with the pains of her past, which held her heart captive. She knew she had to make a decision to call her father and have the conversation that they both had been putting off for a long time.

Daniela sat on the couch in the living room and eyed the cordless phone on the end table as though it were a serpent that would jump to bite her at any moment. Her palms grew sweaty and her throat grew dry as she considered how her father would react to what she had to say. She got up and went into the kitchen and drank water to sooth her dry throat, then she paced up and down the length of her apartment, going over what to say in her mind. Finally, she went back to the living room and sat down. She picked up the phone and with shaky hands, she called her father, breathlessly waiting for him to pick up.

"How are you, Dad?" she said when she heard his voice on the other end.

"I'm doing fine."

"How's Gram?"

"She's doing better."

Daniela gathered her strength in the midst of a lengthy pause. "Dad, we need to talk about what happened with Mom." She looked upward to block the tears that were springing into her eyes. "I know you don't like to talk about it, and neither do I. But we need to discuss this or it will continue to be a problem between us."

When he didn't respond she continued. "I don't understand why you treated her the way you did. How could you be so cruel to her when you were supposed to love her?"

She could hear his long sigh on the other end. "Dani, I cannot take back what has happened and I cannot give you the peace that you want." He cleared his throat. "I have to go."

"Dad, wait. Why can't you just admit what you have done? Do you know that what you did to Mom continues to affect me and any relationship that I had or want to have?"

"I cannot do this now," he said in a hushed and frustrated tone.

Daniela clenched her jaw, her anger producing heat underneath her skin. Before she knew it, she uttered words that she couldn't nor wouldn't take back. "You are a coward, Dad."

Seconds later she was hearing the dial tone as her father had hung up on her. Daniela dropped the phone and covered her face with her hands. She pressed her fingers tightly over her eye, but that did little to block out the image she could never erase from her mind— the image of her mother's cold, lifeless body languishing on the ground clinging to the bloody knife she'd used to snuff out her own life. On that day she lost more than her mother; she lost her will to love.

The day was normal, or at least it seemed that way. She'd entered the house and all was quiet. She'd gone into her grandmother's room to check on her like she always did and found her sound asleep. Tiptoeing out of the room, she went to her own room to put away her belongings. Then she walked into the kitchen and gasped as she spotted her mother on the floor with the knife she used to end her own life still plunged in her chest. There was a pool of blood staining the cottony dress she was wearing. Instinctively, Daniela phoned for help, all the while unwilling or unable to keep her eyes off her mother's face, which was now an unnatural ashen color. Then Daniela returned to her mother's side, the seed of bitterness and anger planted firmly inside her heart.

Chapter 22

Daniela couldn't deny her affections for Micah any longer. She wanted to believe that she could put the past behind her and look forward to a future that they could have together. The day after she spoke with her father, she went to church and spent hours in prayer, asking for help to leave the past behind and for answers regarding her future. She prayed about Micah and she believed she received her answer when she felt led to Psalm 37:23, which reminded her that the Lord directs the steps of those who delight in Him. Determined, she went home that same evening, and after some moments of hesitation, she called Micah.

Her heart sped up when he picked up the phone, and she fumbled for words, wishing she'd rehearsed beforehand what she wanted to say. "I . . . thought we . . . I was hoping you . . . Do you think we could have dinner and talk tomorrow evening if you're not too busy?"

He was silent for a long second. "Are you sure? I thought you wanted to keep things on a friendship level, if we're even that." His tone was low and indignant, and she didn't know how to respond to it.

Daniela tried to swallow the lump that'd formed in her throat. Of course, he was angry with her, and she should've expected it. "I'm sorry," she almost croaked. "I shouldn't have called."

He sighed. "Wait. Can you tell me why you called?"

"I never meant to hurt you," she said. "I'm sorry."

He paused. "What I want to know is why you won't let me in."

Daniela stood up and paced up and down her living room. "It's hard to explain right now . . . over the phone."

"Then have dinner with me," Micah said. "And explain it to me then."

She nodded. "All right, Micah. But dinner will be on me. I'd like to cook and invite you over if you're willing."

"I accept," he said with levity in his tone. "Thank you for trusting me enough to invite me into your home."

"Thank you for accepting my invitation." Daniela smiled.

After pausing, Micah said, "Your invitation means a lot to me, Daniela, and I promise I won't violate your trust in me."

Daniela began the preparations for dinner and dug in her small pantry for all the ingredients she'd need to make a hearty meal of meatloaf, sweet mashed potatoes, and vegetables. After the meal got underway, she quickly tossed together a salad. Then she pondered on dessert. Immediately, she decided on an ice cream cake as a way of commemorating the time that she and Micah had gone to the ice cream shop together. But she needed to head to the supermarket to pick one up.

Daniela drove the short distance to the corner supermarket to pick up the dessert, wanting to rush back and do some sprucing up around the apartment to make sure that it was both spotless and accommodating for Micah. She didn't want him to trip over anything or to get hurt unnecessarily.

Remembering that Micah liked chocolate, she picked out a vanilla and chocolate flavored ice cream cake with confetti-like candy sprinkled over the frosting and brought it to the checkout counter. She got behind a woman who was talking on her cell phone. Absently she looked at the tall, shapely woman with her smart, tailored suit and heard her laughing at something the person on the other line had said.

"I know, girl," the woman responded. "He doesn't know it yet, but you mark my words, we'll be walking down that aisle in no time."

The line was inching upward and Daniela glanced down at her watch. To pass the time, she picked up one of the countless magazines that were shelved along the wire racks near the register and browsed through it. But she quickly snapped to attention when she heard the woman utter a familiar name.

"Did I not tell you that one day I'd be Mrs. Micah Lambert?" the woman said with satisfaction. "Honestly, the blind thing isn't an issue for me, at least not anymore. The man is good-looking and he's successful. What more could a girl want?" She laughed again. "Listen I just got up to the cash register. I'll call you when I'm inside the car. Okay, bye."

Daniela's blood ran cold as though she'd been doused in an ice bath. She was experiencing shortness of breath. The woman had quickly paid for her items and was making her way out of the store. Daniela watched her with a mixture of horror and fascination. When it was her turn to pay for her item she couldn't move, suddenly forgetting what she was supposed to do.

"Hey, are you okay?" the male cashier asked her.

She jerked out of her initial state of shock and abandoned her purchase, ignoring the calls of the dumbfounded cashier and proceeded to follow the woman out the door of the supermarket, all the while wondering what she would say to her when she caught up with her.

"Excuse me," Daniela called out just before the woman got inside her car.

The woman turned around and looked at her curiously, her shapely eyebrows arched. "Yes? May I help you?"

Daniela glanced about her nervously and then pinned her eyes downward as she considered how to proceed. "I couldn't help but to overhear you mention a name in there," she said, looking up and pointing behind her at the supermarket. "You said Micah Lambert and you also mentioned that he's blind, is that correct?"

The woman's expression went from curious to suspicious. "I did, and he is my fiancé. Do you know Micah?"

Daniela's heart sunk. She clenched her jaw tightly and forced herself to remain expressionless. She shook her head at the woman's inquiry and turned quickly and headed toward her car. She hadn't lied since the man she thought she knew was not at all whom she'd expected him to be. Daniela didn't bother to turn back around to see if the woman was still there. She drove the short distance back to her apartment, all the while sniffling back the tears. The image of the woman telling her that Micah was her fiancé taunted her all the way home.

As soon as Daniela walked inside the apartment, the fragrant scent of the dinner she was preparing hit her like a forceful blow to the face and she felt sick to her stomach. She went into the kitchen and turned off the oven. In a daze, she walked into the living room and plopped down on the couch. She placed her hands over her face and her shoulders shook as she cried. "Oh, Lord," she uttered quietly. "How could I be so blind?"

After some time she stiffened and gripped her cell phone and called Micah. She wanted to put an end to their relationship charade before it had even begun.

"It's Daniela," she said when he answered. Her voice sounded lifeless and was unrecognizable even to herself.

"What's wrong?" Micah asked right away. "You don't sound very good."

"Something's come up and I have to cancel our dinner plans." She fought back the tears that were brimming to the surface once again.

"Is there anything I can do to help?"

"No."

You've done enough, she thought. "I have to go. Goodbye, Micah."

She hung up the phone quickly, not giving him a chance to respond. Then she shut her eyes and let the tears fall and wondered how she was going to get him out of her heart.

Micah couldn't put his finger on it but between their dinner plans and that strange phone call he'd received from Daniela, something had changed, and not for the better. After she'd called to cancel their plans he'd been trying to get in touch with her to find out if she was all right, but she wouldn't pick up her phone or return his countless voicemail messages or text messages.

Micah's phone rang and he stopped to pick up the call when the screen reader announced his Uncle Joseph's name. But when he greeted Uncle Joseph there was an unusual pause on the other end of the line.

"It's not your Uncle Jo, Micah. It's your mother."

He tensed up and absently gripped the side edge of the desk in his office.

"I knew you'd pick up the phone if you knew that Joseph was the one calling you."

"Mom," he mumbled. "Is everything okay?"

"Not everything, my son," she said. "I want our family back together again and that can't happen without you." She sighed. "And with Christmas coming soon now is a good time to make the effort. Do you remember how we used to have our Lambert family gatherings every Christmas?"

"How could I forget?" Micah chuckled despite himself. "They were the highlight of the holiday season. We used to gather around and swap stories and gifts, and drink eggnog till we couldn't stomach it anymore. And you insisted that we reflect on the true meaning of Christmas. So we'd gather together and you'd recount the Christmas story like we were all five years old or something."

"And you know you loved every minute of it." Ann Lee Lambert laughed.

Micah paused for a second. "Those were good times, Mom. But they're long gone now."

"But we can salvage the time that we do have. And that's the reason for my call, Micah," she said earnestly. "I want you to be with us this Christmas and to be a part of the family again. I want us to start new traditions together."

"I don't think so, Mom. Too much has happened to make things right between us now." He shook his head firmly. "Besides, my being there would only complicate things."

"It'll never be too late, Micah," his mother insisted. "Do you think it was an accident that you came back into our lives? It was part of God's plan to reunite this family, I'm sure of it. I just need you to try. Come and be with us, and let God complete His work."

Micah sighed. He stood up and placed his hand in his pocket. He rubbed the side of his face. "Let me think about it, okay?"

"All right, my son," she said.

Chapter 23

The only way Micah knew he'd be able to speak with Daniela was if he went to her work. He had to find out what'd happened to cause the rift that was now growing wider between them. With cane in hand, he entered the library and headed toward the circulation desk.

Before he got to the front he could hear her approaching him, her slightly hesitant steps recognizable to him now.

"What are you doing here, Micah?" Daniela asked quietly.

"We need to talk," he said. "Can you take a break and step outside with me?"

"I'm sorry, but I can't."

He pursed his lips, visibly frustrated. "Look, I'm not leaving till you tell me what's happened between us. All of a sudden you're distant again and you're not telling me why. Did I do something wrong?"

Daniela glanced around and spotted a few of her coworkers glancing in their direction. Thankfully, Erin was not in the vicinity. But she knew she needed to end this scene quickly before it got out of hand.

"I have a break in about fifteen minutes," she said. "We can talk then."

❖❖❖

Micah waited outside the library entrance until she emerged. He was relieved when she agreed to sit with him inside the limo so they could speak openly and honestly.

The first minutes were awkward as neither of them spoke. Then Micah cleared his throat and turned to her in earnest. "Tell me what's going on, Daniela," he said. "I thought we were moving toward something real, and then out of the blue you flip out on me. Tell me what the problem is."

She glanced down at her hands, which were folded on her lap, and swallowed back the tears she wanted to shed. "I shouldn't have expected things to be different with us."

"What do you mean?" He knitted his brow confusedly. "Please, talk to me."

"I thought I could trust you, Micah. But I was wrong."

His eyebrows shot up. "When have I given you a reason not to trust me?"

Daniela looked at him and felt the radiant heat of anger coloring her cheeks. "I don't know her name," she said coolly, "but she knew your name very well. In fact, I believe she called you her fiancé." Daniela breathed out to control her voice, which was visibly shaking with emotion. "She's the one you should be sitting in here with and talking to, not me."

Reaching for the door handle of the car, she added, "I have to get back to work. Please don't contact me again," she said. "Goodbye, Micah."

"Wait, Daniela." Micah's voice was strained as he called after her a number of times to no avail. He remained in his seat stunned, trying to make sense of what she'd just told him. It didn't make any sense. Why did Daniela think that he was engaged to be married and who was this mystery woman he was supposed to be engaged to?

Micah sat outside the church building feeling strangely indecisive. Should he listen to his brain and leave or should he submit to this voice inside his heart that was becoming louder with each passing day.

"I can't just sit here," he said. "What would you do if you were me, Mr. Ben?"

"Well," Ben said in his slow and deliberate way. "There are always two choices a person has to make. And one way is generally harder than the other, and that's usually the best way to go because it teaches you an important lesson that you need to know. So I say, think about which is harder to do, staying or leaving. And then do the hardest thing."

Micah sighed. "That's easy, staying is definitely the harder choice."

He wasn't certain why he decided to go to Bethel Baptist Church, except to stage a run-in with Daniela to get her to speak with him. But was that the only reason why he came, or was there a yearning in his spirit that he couldn't contain? The truth was that ever since he'd attended church with Daniela on the Sunday she preached, he'd felt as though it was the opening that God had used to bring him back into fellowship with Him and with other believers. He started praying more and even read his Bible from time to time, and Daniela had a lot to do with that.

Thoughts of her saddened him once more. Before this big misunderstanding about him marrying someone else occurred, they'd crossed an important barrier of trust in their relationship.

Finally, Micah exited the car and Ben led him to the entrance of the church before he retreated back to the car. Though the church's entrance and sanctuary doors were open, the church itself appeared to be empty. There were no sounds but the dull echo of his feet as he walked across the carpeted floor to the doors of the sanctuary.

"Is anyone there?" Micah asked and heard the base of his voice bounce off the walls of the sanctuary.

He sighed and wondered why he was led to be here tonight when obviously there was no service being held. Micah was turning to leave when a familiar voice stopped him.

"Hello, Micah," Daniela greeted him distantly. "I guess you weren't aware that there'd be no prayer meeting tonight. We're having it on Friday instead along with a special Christmas dinner for the homeless."

He nodded, though he was shocked by how God was working His will in their lives once again. "How come you're here by yourself?" Micah asked her.

"I come here often when no one else is around to talk to God and to feel His presence.

"I didn't expect to see you here," she added after an awkward pause.

"I didn't expect to be here." He took a few steps forward. "But my plans were not my own. Mind if I join you?"

"I'm not privileged to say no."

He opted not to respond to her offhanded comment and decided to take a seat in the pew closest to her. He bent his head and prayed before popping his head back up. The tension remained between them, and he wished he could dispel it.

He motioned to speak several times before he forced the words out of his mouth. "When I first lost my eyesight, I used to ask God all the time to give me back what I'd lost, reminding Him of how He gave vision back to the blind all the time in the biblical days."

He cleared his throat. "But soon I learned that there were all kinds of blindness and that seeing people can also be blind, as well. Ignorance is blindness, Daniela. And all the vision in the world can't cure someone if they are blinded to the truth."

"I am not ignorant enough to believe someone who's trying to mislead me." She huffed.

"I would never try to mislead you. And I'd like to clear up this misunderstanding that's gotten between us. But you're running instead of trying to talk this out."

He waited for her to respond, hoping that she would listen to the truth or at least give him an opportunity to defend himself against her accusation.

"There's a conference room outside of the sanctuary," Daniela uttered quietly. "We can talk there."

He nodded with a look of relief replacing his anxious expression.

"Can you please lead the way?" He stood and stretched out his hand as she made her way down the aisle toward him. Hesitantly, she circled his arm

around her own and led them to the conference room.
There, she directed Micah to a seat and then sat across
from him.

Being with him, Daniela felt her defenses breaking
down. Silently, she uttered a desperate plea to stand
her ground. She looked up when Micah calmly
addressed her.

"Can you please tell me why you think I have a
fiancé?"

Daniela sat motionless, her face drawn and her
voice flat. "On the night we were supposed to have
dinner together," she began, "I'd gone to the grocery
store to pick up dessert." She looked up at him feeling
her anger rising once again. "While at the checkout
counter, I stood behind this woman who was talking on
her cell phone. I wasn't really paying much attention to
what she was saying until she mentioned your name."
Daniela stopped once more and clenched her jaw before
proceeding. "She said she was going to be the next Mrs.
Micah Lambert, and said how your blindness isn't an
issue for her since you were good-looking and
successful."

"Can you tell me more about this woman—how she
sounded and what she looked like?"

Daniela let out an exasperated breath. "She had a
Southern accent," she said with a shrug. "She was the
tall, lean, and pretty model type you men like. She had
smooth caramel skin and long, wavy black hair. She
was dressed in a power suit, like she was the CEO of
some company."

"If you're willing to listen I can clear this up right now," Micah told her.

She crossed her arms against her chest. "I'm listening."

Micah gestured with his hand as he began to explain. "I'm positive the woman you saw was Claudia, an old girlfriend from my past. She wants me to give our relationship another try. But there's nothing going on between her and me. Our relationship ended a long time ago, and that's where it's going to stay, in the past."

Daniela lowered her arms and frowned confusedly. "Then why is she talking about marrying you?"

"She's convinced herself that we're going to get married, but I promise you that it's all in her head. I don't intend to marry Claudia. Besides, how could I even consider marrying someone else when you're the one I think about and want to be with?"

Moved by his confession, Daniela's heart stirred within her, awaking from its perpetually dormant state. It glowed inside of her now, its coldness melting like ice dissolving under the warm rays of the sun.

"I want that too," she said softly.

"You do?" A string of emotions were dancing across his face and had registered in his voice.

"Yes." Daniela watched him warily, her nerve endings standing on edge as though she was being pricked by a million pins and needles.

Micah stood up and held out his hand to her. She walked into his willing arms, and he held her in a firm and loving embrace. Then he chuckled aloud and Daniela joined in.

Chapter 24

Daniela was anxious but content as she got ready for the Friday night church service and Christmas dinner at Bethel. She hoped the stirring message that Pastor Sanders had in store would make an impact on the lives of the people they were privileged to serve—the homeless people in their community.

As she made her way out the door, Daniela talked to God in her heart, praying especially for her friend Frances, who had finally accepted her church invitation without much coaxing, and Daniela wanted the message to penetrate her heart and produce a change in her life.

As her talk with God ensued, Daniela admitted she still needed Him to continue to do a work in her as well. Her fears about her growing relationship with Micah were steeped in a past she still hadn't altogether gotten over, especially since it was still the reason she was estranged from her father. Her thoughts of Micah increased as she prepared herself to pick him up so that they could attend the church service together.

"I'm on my way, sweetie." She spoke into the phone as she got inside her car and merged into traffic.

"I'll be outside waiting," Micah responded, the smile apparent in his voice.

They were seated inside the sanctuary and Daniela kept glancing down at her watch, and checking the double doors every so often to make sure she didn't miss her friend's entrance. She hoped Frances hadn't backed out of her promise to attend the service.

"I don't see her yet," she whispered to Micah.

He squeezed her hand encouragingly. "You did your part and invited her. Leave the rest up to God."

"You're right." She squeezed his hand in return.

While the church announcements were being read she looked around at the people in attendance. The church was packed and momentarily she forgot her concerns about her friend's attendance as she considered the many lives that could potentially be impacted that evening.

"Is this seat taken?"

Daniela jumped up and hugged Frances who hugged her back.

When they were seated, she reintroduced Micah to Frances and the two shook hands. Frances smiled at Daniela mischievously and issued her the thumbs up sign. Daniela blushed.

"You've done what few could, Micah, and melted my friend's heart," Frances whispered to him playfully. "She's a tough cookie, that one."

"Free!" Daniela admonished her too loudly and was met with a few looks of disapproval.

Micah chuckled in good-nature.

Thankfully, the praise and worship portion of service began and they ceased talking as they stood up to sing. She and Micah joined right in while Frances took in the atmosphere around her with a stoic expression on her face. Daniela fretted over what she was thinking but decided to leave the results of the evening to God.

"We don't know what tomorrow brings," Pastor Sanders started with no preamble when it came time to ministering the Word of God. "It is not promised to us. What is promised to us is the blessing of a Savior who was born for the purpose of giving us eternal life. He is the risen Lord who took your sins and mine and placed them upon Himself so that we do not have to pay the penalty for our sins, and that is eternal damnation and separation from God."

Pastor Sanders glanced upward and then looked back at the congregation before him. "He did that because He loves us. Many of you are facing terrible trials in your lives right now and you question God's love. But His Word, which comes from Matthew six verse thirty-three, our text for tonight, says, 'But seek first the kingdom of God and His righteousness, and all these things will be added to you.'" He took a step forward and surveyed the congregation before continuing. "The measure of God's love is not in the material possessions that He can provide or in the things that we desire Him to do for us, but it's in the relationship He wants to have with us; the relationship that will guarantee your place in His eternal kingdom; the relationship that will guarantee that you will never be separated from Him ever again.

"Sometimes we become angry and turn away from God when our problems are not taken away from us. But our Lord Jesus died not to give us temporal comfort, but to give us eternal life, which requires fixing our eyes on eternal matters. Our text says seek first His kingdom and righteousness. God will take care of your physical needs, but first your connection with Him and His righteousness is top priority."

The words reverberated with power, and Daniela could feel God's presence in the sanctuary as tears streamed down her face. Micah was also visibly moved as he angled his head upward with a serene expression on his face.

Pastor Sanders issued an altar call and several people moved out of the aisles and made their way to the front of the church. She turned slightly and spotted Frances making her way out of their pew but she grew morose when her friend headed away from the altar and not toward it.

The dinner had been a festive occasion. They had rented out a dining hall a few blocks from the church and had dressed it with Christmas themed decorations like the Nativity scene. They'd also brought in a small Christmas tree and had placed gifts and toys under it for the benefit of the children. People had eaten together in community and laughed, and for the time being had forgotten their troubles. Daniela had been glad to see Micah enjoying himself as he got acquainted with some of the brothers from the congregation. But she'd felt disheartened from the moment Frances had left the service and had not returned.

Now they were heading back to Micah's complex and he discerned Daniela's overwhelming sadness. He turned in her direction from the passenger seat and spoke empathetically.

"Look, sweetheart, it takes time to reach some people." He turned his head toward the passenger side window. "For the longest time, I knew the Lord but I was as distant from Him as an unbeliever because of my anger."

"I just don't want it to be too late for Free, that's all."

"I know." Micah turned his face toward her. "But like I said before, you did your part when you invited Free to the service. Now you have to leave the rest up to God. Besides, think about all the other lives that were saved tonight and give God thanks for that."

Daniela conceded that Micah was right, but that didn't make Frances's disappearing act any easier to take. She wished her friend had at least stayed for the entire program.

"Hey, talk to me," he said, breaking into her thoughts.

"You're right." She threw him a glance and then reached for his hand and squeezed it. "I'm so glad that you're with me, Micah."

He brought her hand to his lips and kissed it. After a while he said, "I hope you'll still think well of me when I ask you for a small favor."

"That doesn't sound so good," she said in good-nature. "But go ahead, I'm listening."

"I want you to go with me to the Lambert family Christmas dinner party this Sunday."

She brought the vehicle to a stop in front of his complex and squinted at him. "You don't think they'll mind me being there?"

"Do you think I care if they do?" he countered with a smile. "Besides, you'll be my guest and not theirs. So say you'll go with me, please?"

"You knew I wouldn't refuse you," she said with a wry smile of her own, "even if you did sneak this up on me at the last minute so that I couldn't refuse."

He chuckled triumphantly. "Good because plan B was to pull out the puppy dog expression."

They laughed and then grew quiet. Micah opened his mouth as if he was about to say something else but decided against it. Instead, he motioned for her to draw closer and he felt for her face, caressing her cheek. He traced her lips with his thumbs, and planted a light kiss there.

"Call me when you get home, okay."

"All right," she replied.

Chapter 25

The air was tense between Daniela and Frances as they sat inside the employee's lounge eating lunch. Daniela kept her eyes pinned to the salad she was moving around on her plate and Frances was munching on the spaghetti dinner she'd brought from home.

"So, we're never talking again?" Frances finally said as she set her fork down and crossed her arms in front of her. "I didn't mean to ditch the service, Dani. But we both know that it wasn't my scene."

"You don't owe me any explanations, Free."

"Apparently, I do since you won't even talk to me. I can see that you're ticked off at me."

Daniela set her own fork down and looked at Frances. She was surprised at what she saw. Underneath the pretty face, the constant smirk, and carefree attitude, was a young woman who looked like she was hurting inside, something Daniela could identify with.

"I'm not angry, Free, just a little disappointed." She managed a smile. "Can you tell me what happened to you? What made you get up and leave like that?"

She sighed. "I don't know." She shrugged. "I guess it got uncomfortable."

"How so?" Daniela got up and advanced closer to where Frances sat. She didn't want to miss an opportunity to minister to her friend if it presented itself. Frances was quiet for a second, glancing down at her food and seeing her past. "Do you remember when the pastor spoke about how we get angry with God for not doing what we want Him to do?" she asked. "He was talking about me."

Daniela listened but said nothing, waiting for her to continue.

"I used to go to church," she said, her mouth turned downward. "I'd be the first one in service and the last one to leave. And I'd read my Bible and pray. Then my mother developed cancer and I prayed and prayed for God to heal her but He didn't and she died. Then my father died soon after and I was left all alone." Her mouth quivered with emotion. "I figured that God didn't care about what happened to me and so I stopped going to church and reading my Bible because none of that mattered to me anymore."

Daniela touched her friend's arm comfortingly. She encouraged Frances to continue, wanting her to release the burden that was in her heart.

"I didn't want to believe anymore. So when the pastor started talking about God's love and how we need to seek Him, I wanted to tune the words out, but I couldn't. And then I felt like crying so I left."

"You were being convicted, Free," Daniela said gently. "That was the Holy Spirit ministering to you."

Frances glanced tiredly at Daniela, her eyes now red and puffy. "What really got to me was when he started talking about the measure of God's love. For the longest I thought that if I were a good Christian and did everything I was supposed to do then God would honor my requests. But that's not how it works, is it?"

"God wants us to seek Him first because He knows that He is all we need," Daniela replied. "He didn't promise that only good things would happen to those who follow Him. In fact, Jesus said that we would have many troubles in this world, and that includes losing people we love." She paused and cleared her throat as she thought about losing her own mother. "But He does promise that He will be with us when those troubles come to us, and that He will supply all of our needs if we seek Him with all our hearts."

As soon as Daniela uttered the last sentence, one of their coworkers stuck her head inside the lounge and addressed them. "I hope you guys are done in here. We have a line of patrons waiting at the desk."

Frances and Daniela stood up and started gathering their belongings.

"I'm not promising anything, but I am willing to listen." Frances smiled ruefully. "I'm even willing to attend another service."

"That's a start." Daniela nodded and returned her smile. "No pressure, okay?"

Frances nodded. As they made their way to the circulation desk, she nudged Daniela. "Don't think I forgot about Micah. I want to know everything."

Daniela laughed. "Of course you do."

Chapter 26

Pastor Sanders had asked Daniela to cite the opening prayer for Sunday morning worship service and willingly she complied. Throughout the service, she had been so taken by the praise and worship and the sermon message that she'd had little opportunity to be nervous about accompanying Micah to his family dinner that evening. But when service ended her nervousness began and she prayed that the evening would go well.

Pastor Goodwin, who'd been eyeing her throughout the service, called to her as she was leaving the church building.

He looked her up and down, shielding his perusal with his long lashes. "I wanted to invite you to brunch so that we can have that chat, Sister Daniela."

"I'm sorry, Pastor. But I have a prior engagement for this afternoon." She turned to leave, but his voice stopped her once more.

"All right then, what I have to say won't take long." He paused and then cleared his throat. "I appreciate your zeal and your willingness to do the Lord's work, Sister Daniela," he said. "But I must tell you that a woman's place is under the headship of her husband and his ministry and not behind the pulpit." He rocked on his heels to accentuate his average height. "Now if you should find a man of God such as me who is already primed for the ministry, it would benefit you greatly. In fact, my hope is that you would join me in my ministerial work, and of course in life. Together, we can do mighty things for God."

Daniela couldn't hide her shock and her mouth gaped open. Had she heard him correctly? Though she tried to maintain her composure, she felt the flush of anger rising to her cheeks and warming her face.

"Thank you for your unsolicited views, Pastor Goodwin," she stated once she found her voice again. "But I choose to listen to God and not to man. I know what He has placed in my heart to do, and I won't let anyone deter me from pursuing His will for my life. And as far as your proposal to join forces in ministry and in life, I wouldn't dream of allowing you to demean yourself to be with the likes of me, so I'll have to say no on both counts. Please excuse me."

"I was just trying to be truthful with you, Sister," he called after her, but she refused to turn back.

While Daniela got ready for her trip to Charleston with Micah, she ruminated over her conversation with Mason Goodwin and fumed. But despite her anger, the encounter evoked the anguish she felt concerning what others had to say about her calling, and also her own doubts about her abilities, which continued to cast a looming shadow over her future.

The phone rang interrupting her thoughts.

"I'm downstairs, sweetie. You ready?" Micah said.

"Yes, I'll be right down."

She gathered her belongings and walked down to the limo.

"Thank you, Mr. Ben," Daniela said to the limo driver, who had the car door open and waiting for her.

"It's my pleasure, Miss." He tipped his hat off to her. She'd grown fond of the elder man who always had a kind word and a sincere smile. Daniela also appreciated how Ben treated Micah, offering fatherly advice and showing him love and support.

"How was service?" Micah asked after giving her a warm hug and kiss. "I'm sorry I couldn't be there with you today."

"Me too," she said, squeezing his hand. "Service was great, as usual. It's what happened afterwards that put a bad taste in my mouth."

"What happened?"

She leaned closer to him and sighed. "Mason Goodwin is what happened. He stopped me after service to tell me how he felt about women preachers."

Micah placed his arm around her shoulder. "What did he say?"

"He basically told me that a woman's place was to be involved in her husband's ministry and not behind the pulpit," she said with a hint of exasperation in her voice. "And this man actually told me that he wants me to partner with him in his ministry as his wife."

She could feel Micah tense up. She placed her head on his shoulder. "Of course I said no on both counts. I also told him that I wasn't going to let anyone deter me from God's purpose for my life."

"Good for you." Micah relaxed and rubbed her shoulder. "There're always going to be people like Mason Goodwin who want to stand in the way of your God-given dreams and aspirations. But keep trusting in God and don't give up." Micah paused and kissed her forehead. "And always know that you have this man in your corner rooting for you."

"Thank you, Micah. That means a lot to me." She popped her head up and looked at his handsome profile. And instinctively, she reached for his face and tipped his head down toward her and tenderly kissed his shut eyelids. "And you're an inspiration to me."

"How do you feel about tonight?" Daniela asked after a while.

"Ask me again when it's all done and over with."

"Tell me about your fondest memory of your family." She squinted at him.

Micah chuckled. "That's easy. Christmas morning was always a festive one at the Lambert house. Everyone came over and we all prayed together. And then we enjoyed this huge breakfast that Mom insisted on cooking with minimal help." His tone was distant as though seeing it all unfold in his mind like a picture show. "Then we gathered around the large Christmas tree in the living room and talked and laughed and drank loads of eggnog and exchanged gifts. And then Mom told the Christmas story."

"That sounds wonderful, Micah," Daniela said with moist eyes. "That's the memory I'd like you to keep in mind tonight, sweetheart. Remember the good times and it'll help you get through this bad one. And who knows, maybe this Christmas will bring good tidings to remember."

"It already has," he said meaningfully and rubbed her shoulder again.

She smiled and silently thanked God for uniting the two of them.

Chapter 27

They reached the Lambert estate and Daniela couldn't help but to be impressed by its vastness, which stretched for miles. She peered in awe at the mansion that stood majestically before them, beautifully adorned with Christmas lights.

"This place is amazing," she whispered to Micah.

He nodded. "I know what you mean."

They linked arms and trudged up the long walkway to the house. They climbed the steps to the large wrap-around porch and rang the doorbell. Micah took a deep breath and Daniela squeezed his arm supportively. The door swung open and Daniela recognized Micah's mother, but now she got a chance to see her more closely. Dressed modestly in a colorful silk dress shirt and slacks, she gave off an air of beauty and sophistication. But her smile was warm and inviting.

"Please come in," she said. Her look became apprehensive as she looked lovingly at Micah. "May I hug my son?" She seemed to be asking for his permission.

Daniela stepped aside as Micah stretched out his arms toward his mother. Ann Lee walked into them and they shared a long, overdue embrace. Her sniffling reflected the emotional impact of the moment. When they parted, Ann Lee Lambert seemed to notice Daniela for the first time. Micah introduced her as his girlfriend and she blushed. Hearing him introduce her in this manner for the first time seemed to solidify their relationship, and Daniela was both excited and anxious about what that meant.

"It's nice to have you here, Daniela," Ann Lee said, giving her an affectionate hug. "Please, make yourself at home."

Ann Lee gripped her son's arm as though they'd never been apart and guided them past the opulent living space and out into the dining hall to where the family had gathered. Daniela glanced around along the way and was certain she could get lost in this house without a roadmap. Upon entering the dining room she tried to quell her nervousness while perceiving that there were at least thirty people in attendance, not counting the children, who had their own separate dining table.

Ann Lee announced their arrival and introduced Daniela to the large gathering. All noises died down as all eyes were on Micah and Daniela who joined everyone at the dinner table. Daniela squirmed in her seat and tried to smile at all of these new faces. Micah sensed her discomfort and searched for her hand. Daniela grasped the hand he was extending toward her and they seemed to draw comfort from one another's touch.

Ann Lee cleared her throat loudly, and Daniela noted her frown, which signaled her displeasure at their unwelcoming behavior. "Micah, we're glad that you and Daniela are here with us," she said. "Isn't that right, everyone?"

❖❖❖

There were murmurs of agreement among the crowd. Micah nodded and tried to smile, but the visible silence of his brother and father was almost too much to bear. He tried to concentrate on eating the bounty in front of him. Though he couldn't see any of it, he certainly could smell the delectable meal, which consisted of the traditional turkey, dressing, roasted lamb, sautéed vegetables, and scalloped potatoes; not to mention the deserts—red velvet cake, sweet potato and pumpkin pies, and his favorite rum cake, which would follow the meal, if there was any room left over in their stomachs.

After a short while Micah set his fork down and decided to try and take the initiative and addressed his brother. "How're you feeling, Mark?" He lifted his head slightly and turned his neck backward and forward unsure of where his brother sat.

"I'm all right," he said stiffly.

Micah nodded. "And you, Dad?"

"I'm just fine," he mumbled noncommittally.

"I want to know how the two of you met," Ann Lee said after a little while of extended silence.

"Me too," Micah's cousin, Robin, said.

Daniela blushed and appeared as if she would indulge them with an answer when her cell phone rang. She apologized and quickly exited the room. Micah was recounting how they met at the library when Daniela returned with a crestfallen expression on her face.

"Honey, is something wrong?" Micah's mother asked Daniela.

Micah turned in her direction. "What's going on?"

"I have a family emergency and I'm going to have to leave," she said for the benefit of everyone. "Thank you very much for your hospitality and for a great dinner."

Micah stood up also and searched for Daniela's hand. "I have to take Daniela home." Then he addressed his mother. "Thank you and I'll call you."

"I'm sorry I'm taking you away from your family dinner," Daniela mumbled as she and Micah stepped out into the cool night air and headed toward the limo.

"That's not important right now," he said. "Tell me what's going on."

Inside the limo Daniela sat in a daze staring out the window. She began to feel the familiar tightness in her stomach and the fears that were associated with the events of the past, and once again she questioned who she was inside. She was being pulled back into a past that, for a time, seemed to be growing dim while the future was looking more certain. Perhaps it had all been an illusion, her and Micah. Perhaps, she would never break free. Daniela sighed and rubbed her face, her eyes wet with tears.

She watched vaguely as Micah put up the window that separated the front and back seats of the limo to give them more privacy.

"Are you going to tell me what's going on?" he asked her again.

"It's my father," she said without looking in Micah's direction. "He was admitted to the hospital today after complaining of chest pains."

"I'm sorry, sweetheart," he said.

She balled her hands into fists on her lap. "I should've listened to my instincts and moved back home to be with them." Daniela shook her head in frustration. "I knew he needed me. But I've been so angry with him for so long."

"Look, you can't blame yourself for this. I mean that's what trusting God is all about, right? Turning things over to Him and letting Him work it out."

He reached for her and obligingly she moved closer to him. Micah placed his arm around her shoulder. She shut her eyes and let the tears slide down her cheeks.

"He used to beat her—my mother," she said quietly. "And one day she couldn't take the beatings or the humiliation anymore and she ended her own life." Daniela pulled away from Micah and wiped at her tears. "And even now after learning what just happened, it's hard for me to forgive and forget what he did to her."

Micah furrowed his brow, momentarily stunned into silence. "Why didn't you tell me about this before?"

She turned her head toward the window. The night, which had started out so promising, was turning into a veritable nightmare and she longed to see it end. Daniela's chin quivered with emotion as she tried to compose herself. "It's not something I like to talk about or to remember."

"Maybe you need to talk about it," he said gently.

Micah had always been transparent with her about his past and present battles, and Daniela knew she owed him the same consideration, though now she couldn't help but to feel anxious as she spoke about the ugly truth surrounding her family's history.

"I have a generational curse in my family, Micah." Daniela absently wiped her palms onto the lap of her pants as though she were trying to clean off dirt from her hands. "It's the curse of domestic violence."

Her father had grown up to see his mother being abused by his own father, who was a farmhand during the era of dictatorship in Haiti. He grew angry and frustrated when he couldn't provide for his family; and he took it out on them.

"Gram said it was shame that made him act the way he did, and she tried to endure it hoping that one day he would see that the house was truly a home because of the people inside and not for how big or small it was.

"But he never learned that lesson. He thought that being a man meant putting fear into everyone around you," Daniela said with a hint of bitterness in her tone. "He thought fear was the same as respect."

Gram explained that when he was only seven years old her son, Marcel, Daniela's father, saw his father dragging her across the dirt floor of their hut and he ran up to him with small, balled up fists crying and pleading for him to stop.

"But my grandfather pushed him aside and knocked him down to the ground. Then he pointed his finger at him with a scowl on his face and said, 'When you're older, you will understand that this is how you rule your home, or you will lose control and have a woman rule over you, which will be to your shame.'"

Daniela grunted. "My father must've treasured those words in his heart because when he married my mother, he continued the legacy of violence in his own home."

"And that explains why it's been so hard for you to trust someone with your heart, afraid that the violence will continue with you," Micah said.

She nodded and then cleared her throat. "Yes, my solution was to abstain from relationships at all costs," she said with a rueful smile. "But I never thought I'd meet someone who made me reconsider my position."

"That's a good thing." He reached for her face and caressed it. "You know I'd never hurt you, right, at least not intentionally."

Daniela didn't respond and Micah asked the question again, emphasizing every word.

"Yes, Micah, I believe you," she said distantly.

"Good," he said with apparent relief in his voice. He searched for her hand and gripped it. "How can I help?"

"There's nothing you can do," she said tiredly. "I'm going to have to face this on my own."

"Why do you have to handle this alone?" he asked. "Why won't you let me help you?"

"This has nothing to do with you, Micah."

"It has everything to do with me, Daniela." He sighed. "I'm the man who wants to love you and not hurt you. Don't make me pay for what happened in the past."

She didn't respond.

"I just don't want you to turn back when we've come so far."

"I'm not," she replied in a defenseless tone.

They settled into a noisy silence until the limo reached Daniela's apartment building.

"I'll be taking the earliest flight out to Miami," she said to him. "I'll call you when I get there, okay?"

Micah didn't respond and Daniela sighed resignedly. She reached over and kissed his cheek. But before she could exit the vehicle, Micah reached for her. He pulled her into a tight embrace.

"I'm here for you," he whispered against her ear. "Please don't forget that."

She nodded, unable to speak. Pulling away quickly, Daniela descended the limo before she was tempted to remain in his arms indefinitely.

Chapter 28

With a heart as heavy as her laden steps, Daniela retrieved her suitcase from the baggage carousel and walked outside the doors of the busy terminal in Miami. She rarely traveled by plane, and tried to orient herself as she searched for her cousin, Therese's burgundy Mazda through the line of cars driving by. When she heard a honk, she turned around and saw Therese waving at her. Daniela walked swiftly to the car, dispensed her small luggage in the trunk, and then got inside the car. They barely embraced before being rushed off by airport security.

They were silent for a short time as Therese drove smoothly along Interstate 95. Daniela's head was turned toward her passenger side window and she looked out at the tall buildings that comprised downtown. Her eyes were glazed over with unshed tears. Therese reached out and gripped her hand, squeezing it encouragingly.

"How is Gram doing?"

"She's trying to be strong, but I can tell this is hard for her. She's currently with my parents while your father's in the hospital."

Daniela nodded and sighed. Tired, she tilted her head back against the headrest. "I don't know what I'm going to say to him. I want to be able to support him through this without the anger and bitterness I still feel inside."

"I know," Therese said. "But you know what to do—pray and let God work on your heart. He can remove the things that we can't."

Daniela nodded without comment. She'd barely prayed since this whole ordeal started. "Do you mind driving straight to the hospital?"

"All right," Therese said, and took the exit that would take them to General Hospital.

Minutes later they were trudging through the halls of the hospital floor, and Daniela was unconsciously squeezing the vase of flowers and balloons that she had purchased at the gift shop for her father. He turned his head slightly when they walked into the room.

Daniela bit the inside of her lip to keep from crying out in anguish as she observed the machines that were hooked up to her father. She etched toward him and kissed him, the gesture stiff and awkward.

"You did not have to come all this way for me," he said weakly.

She set the vase on his dinner table. "I wanted to come," she said quietly. "How are you feeling?"

He turned his head away. "I don't feel anything right now."

Daniela glanced at Therese who shook her head regretfully.

"I want to pray for you, Dad," she said in a quiet voice. "Will you let us?"

"I cannot stop you," he mumbled.

Daniela and Therese joined hands and quietly prayed for her father's healing. But silently Daniela prayed for the healing she needed to be able to forgive her father. When they concluded the prayer, she seemed to exhale for the first time.

Micah dragged himself up to a sitting position on the bed and wiped sweat from his brow and upper lip. Like many times before, he found himself awakened from a fitful sleep and greedily gasping for air as though he were suffocating. He pushed his head down between his propped up knees and waited until his breathing evened out. No longer able to go back to sleep, Micah got up and reached for his cane. He went into the kitchen to get a cold glass of water. Soon, thoughts of Daniela were pervading his spirit. They'd spoken after she'd arrived in Florida and she'd given him a recap of her father's condition. They'd prayed together over the phone, but he couldn't squelch the feeling that this separation would cause the demise of their relationship, though at the same time acknowledging that he needed to continue building his faith.

Micah forced the thought away as he made his way back to his room. He settled back on the bed and tried to get some sleep, but was jarred out of a drowsy state by the ringing of his cell phone, which he kept positioned close to his nightstand.

He groaned when he heard the announcement of who the caller was and considered not answering the phone. Against his better judgment, Micah answered Claudia's call.

"You do realize what time it is?" he said in greeting.

"But we haven't talked in forever, sugar. And I wanted to hear your voice. Was that so wrong of me?"

"No one's voice sounds good at one o'clock in the morning, Claudia."

"As I recall, you and I made good use of this time." She laughed seductively. "Sleep was the farthest thing from our minds."

"I'm not amused, Claudia," Micah responded gruffly.

"And I'm not going to deny my feelings for you, Micah. And I'm not going to let you keep putting things off between us. You know that we belong together." She paused to let her words sink in. "I want us to get together to talk about our future, and I'm not taking no for an answer."

Micah rubbed the back of his neck and sighed. They really did need to talk since he'd never confronted her about the conversation that Daniela had overheard at the store. Also, he needed to be upfront with her and put an end to this illusion she had about their having a future together.

"You're right," he said soberly. "How about we meet on Friday night?"

"Great," she voiced in triumph. "I'll be ready when you come to pick me up."

Chapter 29

Daniela had only been in Florida for three days but it felt more like three weeks. She fought exhaustion as she sat beside her father's bed and tried to engage him in conversation.

"I spent some time with Gram, yesterday," she said. "She wishes that she could come and see you, but her health is still too fragile. She wanted me to tell you that she's praying for you."

Her father barely nodded and didn't comment. He had turned his face away from her and was gazing out of the window across the room.

After a few more times of trying, Daniela let out a frustrated breath and stood up abruptly. "I am trying, Dad. Why don't you try too?"

He finally turned his face toward her, and she was surprised to see the tears glistening in his eyes. He didn't bother to wipe them away when they fell out of the corner of his eyes.

Daniela couldn't recall the last time she saw her father cry, and the sight of it began to chip away at her anger. Instinctively, she went into the bathroom and grabbed some tissues. Then she went up to him and proceeded to wipe his tears away. While she tended to him, he gazed up at her with a pained expression on his face.

"You are as beautiful as your mother was, Dani," he mouthed, his voice scratchy and low.

The words brought tears to her own eyes.

"I know you have wanted to talk about your mother and I refused to do so," he said in a stronger tone of voice. "But now it is time."

Daniela went back to her seat, her heart suddenly beating faster in anticipation of what he would say. Now that she would get her wish and hear her father's confession, she wondered if she were better off staying in ignorance of it all. Regardless, he seemed to need to remove this burden that'd no doubt put a strain on his failing heart and the least she could do was to listen to what he had to say.

He said he did not want to make excuses for what he had done. For the time had come when he had to face his own punishment for the suffering he had inflicted on others, especially her mother.

He himself had grown up in a home where he'd seen his father beat his mother like she was his child instead of his wife. And he'd promised himself he would never do the same thing to his wife when he grew up.

"But I was wrong," he said with a long sigh. "I had inherited his poisonous anger and did not know it until the day your mother made me so angry that I hit her for the very first time."

Daniela looked down at her hands, wringing them on her lap as she envisioned the story in her mind. It was both fascinating and frightening.

"She had not done anything to deserve it." Her father lifted his arm up limply and then set it down. "We had gone out together and a man had looked in her direction and smiled." He paused to catch his breath.

"By the time we got home I was so angry I could have wrecked the whole house. Instead, I turned on her and hit her for the first time and then warned her never to let me see a man smile at her like that again."

Daniela squinted at her father and realized that he was getting very tired. "You don't have to say anymore," she said. "You need to get your rest right now. We can speak about this another time."

His mouth trembled slightly. "I know it is too late for apologies," he said in a low whisper. "But I hope that one day you will realize just how sorry I am for everything."

"I'll return soon." She turned around abruptly and left the room unable to hear the rest of his apology.

Daniela walked swiftly to the hospital parking lot, got inside her rental car, and put her head down on the steering wheel. She'd rented a car so she'd have the freedom to come and go as needed without burdening her cousin; and now she was thankful for the solitude so she could break down in private. Her father just made his soul confession and she was angry and grieved for him at the same time. His heartfelt plea for forgiveness was the last thing she'd expected and now she knew she had to forgive him and then seek to forge a relationship they'd never had, one of love and trust. Daniela also knew that she couldn't leave him now and in her mind she'd already decided to move back to Florida to be with him and her grandmother.

Chapter 30

Daniela was in her old bedroom staring at the telephone and willing herself to make the difficult call she didn't want to make to Micah. She looked upward and sought the Lord for strength, and then steadied her nerve and dialed his number.

"Tell me what's going on," he said as soon as he answered the phone. "Is there any improvement in his condition?"

"Not really," she answered wearily. "They're monitoring his heart rate very closely."

"Don't lose hope, all right?" he said. "What about you—how are you holding up?"

"I've been better." She tried to smile. "I know that I have to be strong for him. He's always displayed this tough exterior, and now it's hard to see him looking so vulnerable."

"I wish I could be there with you, sweetheart," Micah said in an earnest voice. "Is there anything I can do to help make this easier for you?"

"Pray," she whispered. "Please pray for him."

"I'll be the first to admit that I've been struggling with my faith for a long time, but now I can see what God can do when we trust Him. When Mark was in that coma, you had faith to believe that he would pull through. Don't lose that," Micah said. "If God can heal my brother, I'm sure He can heal your father too."

"Thank you for reminding me of that." Daniela paused and took a deep breath. She knew that what she planned to say next would wound Micah. But it had to be said and she couldn't put it off any longer. "Micah, I've decided to stay in Florida for a while until my father regains his strength. That way I can also look after my grandmother too."

She cringed at the silence on the other end of the line. "I know this appears to be a sudden move," she went on, "but I've been agonizing about moving back for a long time. And my father's illness just confirmed for me that this is where I need to be right now."

"I understand what you're trying to do, Daniela. But think about the fact that everything you've worked hard for and you're aiming to accomplish is in Charlotte. Are you willing to forgo all of it?"

She sighed. "If I have to, I could continue with school through the distance learning program. I can find work here. And though I'll miss my church home, I can always go back to the church I grew up attending as a child—Gram's church."

"What about you and me?" he said in a low tone. "What's your solution for us?"

She placed her free hand over her face wearily. "I don't know, sweetheart. I'm trying to do what I think is best under these circumstances."

"That's not good enough, Daniela, and you know it."

"I don't see any other way, Micah."

"How about you let me help you with your father and your grandmother," he said. "Just say the word and I'll have your father placed in the best facility here in Charlotte and your grandmother can get the best care around the clock. We both know I have the resources to do it."

"Sweetheart, I can't let you do that." She shook her head stoutly. "I appreciate the offer but this is something I have to take care of on my own."

"I thought we were on this journey together, or was I wrong?"

"I'm sorry, but this is how it has to be for now."

His brooding silence spoke volumes to Daniela, and she knew Micah well enough to know that he was clenching his jaw tightly and succumbing to his anger.

"I think maybe this is how you want it to be," he finally said in a gruff tone. "You're running again, Daniela. And it doesn't look like there's much I can say to stop you."

"You're wrong, Micah," she said with a quiver in her voice. "The truth is I'm running back to a past that's brought me nothing but pain, but I have to do it."

When he didn't reply she looked down at the phone and realized that Micah had hung up on her. Daniela fell back against her bed and tossed the phone aside. She didn't have the energy to scream so she settled for a low groan. Why did he have to make things so difficult?

Her cell phone rang almost immediately after Micah hung up on her. Daniela wasn't going to pick it up, but when she glanced down at the screen, she saw Frances's number and answered the call.

"How's your father?" Frances asked after they'd exchanged greetings.

"He's still in the hospital," she responded with a weighty sigh. "And it looks like he'll be there for a while."

"I'm so sorry, Dani."

After the slightest hesitation, Daniela blurted out, "I'm not coming back, Free. I've decided to stay in Florida to help my dad and grandmother."

Frances was silent for a long moment. "You must do what you feel is necessary," she said finally. "I'm going to miss you, kid. It won't be the same here without you."

Daniela swallowed back her sobs. "I'm going to miss you too, my friend."

"Have you already spoken with Erin?" Frances asked.

"Yes, I called her earlier today." Daniela recalled how surprised she was at their supervisor's empathetic attitude. "She said she understood my decision and even offered to give me a letter of recommendation," she added.

"Well, what do you know? Maybe she does have a heart after all." Frances paused. "Listen, I know that you trust in God, so don't lose faith now, okay?"

Daniela's eyes widened slightly registering her surprise at her friend's spiritual statement. "Thank you, Free."

After hanging up with Frances, Daniela set the phone down and rubbed her face tiredly. But there was no rest for the weary, and she knew that if she kept moving she wouldn't have to think about her conversation with Micah and everything else that seemed to be going wrong around her. She sought the will to keep moving, and soon she was on her way back to the hospital.

Although her father had been previously moved out of the intensive care unit, Daniela learned that her father's doctor had ordered him to be moved back into the ICU with around the clock medical attention. When she was permitted to see him, she sat with him and anxiously inspected his every movement. At one point he awoke and stirred around the bed, causing one of the monitors to sound off. Daniela stood up abruptly, panic-stricken. The night nurse briskly walked into the room, quieted the monitor, and gave her father a sedative which calmed him down. Soon after, he fell into a fitful sleep.

Daniela didn't realize it when she dozed off herself until she was awakened by a gentle hand clasping her shoulder.

"You need to go and get some rest, sweetheart," her Aunt Sylvie said in her familiar, soft, silky voice.

Daniela stood up and hugged her aunt whose portly figure and inquisitive eyes were a replica of her grandmother's. She looked over at her father. His eyes were shut, but his lips were moving slightly as though he were having a conversation with someone in his sleep.

"He's so fragile now, Auntie." Daniela shook her head. "I never thought my father would look so helpless."

Aunt Sylvie followed her gaze. "Go rest; I will stay with him."

"I don't want to leave him."

"Then do it as a favor to me. I want to spend a little time alone with my brother."

Solemnly, Daniela nodded. She walked over to her father and kissed him lightly on his cheek. She gave her aunt a quick hug before exiting the room.

As soon as Daniela got to her father's house, she barely freshened up before plopping down onto the bed and losing consciousness. She was roused out of sleep by the shrill ringing of her cell phone. Disoriented, she sat up and looked around for it.

"Hello," she mumbled into the phone after she took it from her purse, which was perched up on the nightstand.

"Dani, come to the hospital right away."

Now fully awake, her heart lurched in her chest. "What is it, Aunt Sylvie? What's wrong?"

"It is not good; please come." She hung up the phone before Daniela could probe her any further about her father's condition.

Blindly, Daniela grabbed her purse and rushed out of the house. Inside the car she alternated between praying and sobbing.

It was nine o'clock in the evening. She bypassed the local routes and took the highway which would get her to the hospital the fastest. When she got there, she didn't bother to park the car, leaving it at the front entrance. She rushed toward the elevators, barely containing her frustrations as it took its time getting up to her father's floor.

As soon as she exited the elevator, she was met with her aunt whose face was now stained with tears. Daniela's knees buckled and she fell to the ground. Her aunt didn't have to say a word. She already knew that her father was dead.

She didn't make an effort when her aunt tried to pull her up off the floor. She leaned against her like dead weight and sobbed into the folds of her cottony dress. Her head throbbed and the only coherent thought that filtered through her brain was the fact that she hadn't gotten the chance to say goodbye.

Chapter 31

"How did this happen?" Micah demanded to know. "And who authorized you to make these changes?"

The employee was dumbfounded and remained mute while Micah issued his reprimand, the bass of his voice making him sound even more menacing. Micah got up from his desk and leaned forward, burrowing his fists on top of the piles of paper on his desk.

"I don't care how you do it, but this mistake had better be rectified right now or someone's going to pay. Now get it done and get back to me."

The employee rushed out of the office and almost knocked Ace over along the way.

Gingerly Ace knocked on Micah's door to alert him of his presence, and then stepped inside his office, closing the door behind him.

"What's up, man?" he asked. "I could hear you from down the hall."

Micah shook his head and plopped down in his seat. "I'm fine," he bellowed.

"Yeah, I can see that," Ace responded dryly.

Micah blew out an exasperated breath. "Look, I got a lot on my mind, that's all."

"I think you need to get away from this place, Micah, my man," Ace said. "The day is almost done anyway. If you're up for it, we could stop by the gym and get a workout in; that's always a great way to release some stress."

"I think you're right." Micah nodded. "Sounds like a plan."

An hour later Ace was escorting Micah to a local gym located within walking distance from the office building. They would go there from time to time. Micah was familiar with the layout, which helped him to maneuver around to his favorite machines with minimal help.

Micah took in his environment with his keen senses. The gym sounded relatively crowded and the smell of fragrance mixed with perspiration spoke of the energy that permeated through the atmosphere. Suddenly he was charged and ready to go. He and Ace always kept gym clothes at work for occasions like this one.

They were pedaling on adjacent bikes for about half an hour without speaking. Micah was glad that Ace was giving him the courtesy of time without pressuring him to talk. He halted his motion on the bike and let his breathing even out before he spoke up about what was bothering him.

"I just found out that I may be losing the woman who I thought was the one for me."

"That's rough, man." Ace slowed down his peddling. "But if she's the one God has for you, she won't get away."

"I wish I had your faith."

Ace smiled. "It's not only faith talking, Micah. It's experience. Did I ever tell you that Tonya and I almost didn't get married?"

"No." He frowned. "Tell me what happened."

Ace stopped pedaling and cocked his head to the side as he recalled the past. "She'd been offered this dream job in Detroit and ultimately decided to take it." He shook his head. "Of course, I blew up at her and accused her of trying to sabotage the good thing we had going."

"How did she respond?" Micah prompted when he paused.

"It made her mad and more determined to go," he said matter-of-factly. "Of course that made me angrier and we broke things off." He sighed. "I was miserable and really started praying about us, reminding God that He was the one who brought us together, and though we didn't always do things His way, He was a forgiving God and could mend our broken relationship."

Micah continued to listen intently, realizing once again that Ace had a gift of bringing a godly perspective to situations and Micah was beginning to see his own predicament with fresh eyes through Ace's story.

"And He spoke to my heart," his friend continued, "and told me to do the hardest thing I ever had to do, let her go." Ace smiled ruefully. "The Lord made me realize that since He's the One in charge, it would all work out and that Tonya and I would be together since it was His plan for us. But I had to stop fighting her and stop fighting God to try to get my own way.

"So I let her go. After a few months apart, she shows up on my porch with tears in her eyes. She told me that her home was wherever I was. I pulled her close to me, and we've never been apart since."

Micah was quiet for a time, feeling the tug of conviction in his heart. "So you're saying that I shouldn't fight Daniela on this because God will work things out between us. I just need to give her and Him the time to do it."

"I'm glad to know you were listening," Ace said good-naturedly.

"Ace, man, you should be at some office somewhere charging fifty-dollars an hour for the Christian counseling that you're doling out for free."

Ace laughed. "No, man, I'm happy right where I am, and doing what I do. But if you should want to give a brother a little raise, I won't be mad at you."

"You may just get your wish," Micah said, joining in his laughter.

Micah had to shake his head in utter amazement. If he'd had any lingering doubts about God's power to bring people together, they were effaced as he marveled at the person who was now standing outside his door. He ushered his visitor in, and they stood silently for what seemed like a long time with neither one of them venturing to speak. Finally, he cleared his throat and tried to be the dutiful host.

"Would you like something to drink?"

"No thanks," Mark replied.

Micah offered his brother a seat, and then he sat across from him on the living room couch. There was an air of tension and discomfort between them but at least they were sitting down together and talking, which was more than he'd ever hoped for. After a few minutes of awkward silence, Micah braved going beyond surface talk and got to the heart of the matter between them. He leaned forward, resting his elbows above his knees.

"I was hoping for this day, Mark." He felt his throat constrict with rawness of emotion as he cleared it and continued. "A time when we could try and get past all this anger between us and talk one on one."

"If that's true then why didn't you try to contact me and make it happen?"

Micah tilted his head down. "I wanted to so many times, but it's always easier to do the wrong thing, than to do what's right." He lifted his head up and rubbed his palms together pensively. "When I left home, I didn't want to turn back. I associated it with all the bad stuff that happened and I didn't want to go back there again."

"So I was a reminder of the bad stuff you wanted to leave behind," Mark said flatly. There was a hint of pain in his voice.

"That's how it felt at the time," Micah said in a low tone. "But now I realize that this is the way it needed to be all along. I had to leave in order to become the person I was meant to be."

Mark scoffed. "You know, I used to tell myself that you'd died. That way I didn't have to wonder where you were."

Micah swallowed the lump in his throat. "Was that what you wanted, for me to be dead?"

"I wanted you to be around," Mark said in a raised voice. "I wanted the brother I grew up with who was my best friend."

Micah felt a stab in his heart. "I'm sorry, Mark."

"How could you just leave like that?"

Micah got up from the couch and ambled toward the large wall to ceiling window in the living room. "You see the scene out there?" He used his cane to point at outside. "I used to regret I was ever born because I couldn't see it anymore." Micah kept his face hidden as he spoke. "But worse than how I felt about myself was how you guys viewed me. I became the useless invalid, the one everyone tiptoed around, and worse, the burden of the family."

"You were never a burden to anyone but yourself, Micah. You chose to leave."

Micah whirled around. "You took my place, Mark. Do you know how painful that was for me to witness? Everything that was supposed to be mine was taken from me. And there was nothing I could do about it. Do you have any idea how betrayed I felt?"

Mark didn't respond. They were quiet for a long, tense minute, and then Micah sighed and walked back to the couch and sat down.

"I left, Mark, because I wanted to prove that even I could be something beyond what other people thought I could be." He shook his head. "But I've been wrong on so many levels. For one thing, God has changed me in so many ways. He's made me realize that what's important in life is His will and not mine or anyone else's. I don't want to waste any more time fighting about what doesn't matter. I'd like us to move forward, if you're willing."

Mark was silent for a moment. Then he said, "I'd like that."

Smiling, Micah stood up and extended his hand toward his brother.

Mark stood up and slowly made his way toward Micah. He reached for the hand Micah was extending and shook it.

Then instinctively they drew in and placed an arm around each other.

Chapter 32

Micah tried calling Daniela again; the phone went straight to voicemail as before. Micah knew he had to keep trying to get in touch with her to make sure that she was all right. He'd had a disturbing dream the night before that'd left a bad taste in his mouth, and he was certain it was true, though praying that it wasn't. Her father had died.

He'd called her countless times since their unpleasant phone conversation more than a week before, and he'd concluded that she didn't want to be reached. Micah couldn't blame her for being angry with him. In retrospect he'd acted selfishly when she'd needed his support the most. But now all he wanted to do was to speak with her and to offer her all of the support and encouragement she needed to get through this difficult time.

After work one evening, he dialed her number again and was set to leave another message on her voicemail, when surprisingly she picked up the phone.

"How are you?" he asked her anxiously.

"My father's gone," she said in a deadened voice.

He made a head nod motion as she confirmed what he already knew. "I don't have the words that can take away your pain," he said. "But I'll listen if you want to talk about it."

She was quiet for a long time, and then sniffled as though suddenly overcome by emotions she'd been trying to hold in. "I don't understand why it had to happen now," she said in a strained voice. "Just when he and I were making an effort to have a relationship."

"I'm sorry." Micah wanted to say more but he was certain that anything he said wouldn't be enough to lessen the burden of her loss, so he contented himself with waiting for her to voice her affliction.

"Thank you." She was quiet for a little while, and he could hear her soft breathing over the phone. "I'm glad we managed to make peace with each other before he died," she said in a soft voice. "I just hope that he made peace with God. I prayed for him and with him."

"You did what you could. You have to leave the rest up to God."

She didn't reply.

"How can I help?" Micah asked.

"Will you pray with me?"

"Sure, I can do that."

He remained silent while she prayed. Afterwards he spoke words he hoped would sooth her soul. "You're not going through this alone. Just know that I'm thinking of you, all right?" He cleared his throat. "And also know that I love you."

She gasped slightly and then sniffled as fresh tears began to cascade down her cheeks. Anxiously, he called out her name.

"I love you, too," she managed to say in a muffled voice.

Chapter 33

Micah was starting to see God in the small things now, like in the way He'd expanded his capacity to love more selflessly. He carried Daniela's grief as though it was his own, and Micah prayed constantly for her. Though he wanted her to return so they could become fully committed to one another, he was willing to wait for her for as long as it took. He also knew that in order for things to work between them, he needed to settle things with Claudia once and for all.

On the Friday, he and Claudia were scheduled to meet. He picked her up and took her to dinner. Micah did not go to her favorite restaurant since he wanted to make it clear to her that they were not there to celebrate a reunion, but rather to negotiate a parting of ways. Instead, he chose a classic, though less formal and less intimate, Italian restaurant in uptown Charlotte. It was clean and comfortable with a casual feel and the dinner menu was eclectic.

"I guess this'll do," Claudia commented doubtfully as they took their seats.

"It's not your usual style, but it's a good spot." Micah smiled thinly. Inwardly, he was mulling over the things he wanted to say to her. He waited until they were served and had started eating before he revealed what was on his mind.

"You've been an important part of my life, Claudia," he said. "And it's not my intention to hurt you."

"But...," she prodded as she squinted at him.

"But it's time to accept the fact that our relationship is over."

"And this is because you're so in love with your mystery woman, right?"

"This is about you and me, Claudia. So please leave Daniela out of this." He pushed back in his seat and crossed his arms over his chest. "I've always tried to be upfront with you about how I felt about us, and about my feelings for someone else."

Claudia leaned backward and crossed her arms with indignation. "You've never spoken her name before till now. Maybe she is real after all. Do you love this Daniela?"

"That's not your concern," he said.

"So you expect me to quietly step aside while you romance some other woman."

"Let's not do this, Claudia."

Tossing her napkin aside Claudia pushed back her chair and stood up. "You're the one who needs to stop, Micah, before you throw away a chance to have what we both want, a lifetime of happiness together."

"Like I said before, things changed between us and we don't want the same things." He paused before continuing, "It's not about what you want from the other person. It's about what you're willing to give to the other person. It's about seeing someone for who they are instead of what you want them to be. It's about making the decision to stay, even when you want to go, because you made a commitment to the person and not to a lifestyle." Micah took a deep breath. "I've moved on, Claudia, and you should too."

"You're just saying that—" she said as she stroked the side of his cheek.

"Goodbye, Claudia." Micah turned away from her touch.

Livid, Claudia cursed under her breath, and stomped away from the table, making sure he could hear the clicking of her heels as she departed. *He's rejecting me? Who does he think he is?* she thought as she determinedly made her way through the restaurant's front door and quickly secured her own transportation home.

Chapter 34

Daniela forced herself to conduct the difficult task. Though she'd been avoiding it since the funeral, she knew she had to put her father's things in order. She wandered into his room, looking around in a daze as though she were seeing strange artifacts inside of a museum while lightly touching some of his belongings. Daniela opened the door to his closet and surveyed his familiar shirts and slacks. It was hard to believe that he was gone and would never come back. She shut her eyes and tried to summon her strength to continue working. With a determined expression on her face, she began to pack her father's belongings to place in storage or to give to those in need. Daniela sang hymns while she worked to keep her mind focused on God and not on the lonely and empty feeling that was sitting in the pit of her stomach.

Afterwards, she drove to her Aunt Sylvie's house to visit with Gram, the only other person who understood the pain that accompanied her loss.

Along the way Daniela perused the familiar streets of Miami, and saw the dual effects of the richness and poverty of the local town she'd called home for so many years. She watched the slow and steady move of people walking about the streets, the diverse businesses along each corner, the cracked pavements and dirty sidewalks, and she was struck with nostalgia. These were the same streets that she'd known when both her mother and her father lived, and though they were still the same, somehow they were different now; it was like looking at the world from the wrong end of a telescope—it looked small and unfocused.

Once she'd made her way inside her aunt's suburban neighborhood, Daniela parked the car in the empty driveway and used the key that was under the mat to open the front door. She made her way up the stairs to the guest bedroom that her grandmother occupied and knocked before entering. Gram was sitting in a chair, staring out the window. She turned in her direction with a distant look. Daniela walked up to her and hugged her. Then she kneeled in front of her and took hold of her hand.

"How are you feeling, Gram?" Daniela asked gently.

"I feel like I am alive outside but dead inside." She shrugged. Her eyes were swollen and red from crying. "It is true what they say, that parents shouldn't outlive their own children."

Daniela said nothing as she squeezed her grandmother's hand comfortingly. Gram turned to her and smiled sadly.

"I am sad for another reason too," she said.

Daniela frowned and waited for her grandmother to speak.

"I know that it is time for you to leave, Dani."

Daniela got up and walked over to the window, crossing her arms as she leaned against the wall. "I don't want to leave you."

"It is time for you to live the life that God intended for you, sweetheart." Gram's tone was resolute. "You must look ahead to the future."

"Maybe my future is here, to take care of you."

"I will remain with your Aunt Sylvie, and you will return where you belong to do the work that God has called you to do."

"I'm not sure I want to go back," Daniela said in a low tone.

"Come and sit beside me, Dani."

Dutifully, she went and retrieved a folding chair in the room and placed it beside her grandmother. Gram gripped her hand.

"The Lord is with you, my child, so do not be afraid. You only have to trust that He is guiding you wherever you go and whatever you do."

Although Daniela realized her grandmother was right, the sensation that was running up and down her spine was fear of what waited for her in Charlotte. Her ministry goals, her vocational career as a pastor, and her relationship with Micah produced hope, but also came with difficulties that she wondered if she were ready to commit to.

When the nurse's aide came to assist her grandmother, Daniela helped put her to bed and remained with her until Gram fell asleep.

Daniela drove back to her father's house in deep thought, mulling over her conversation with her grandmother. She parked in front of the driveway and stared at the house she associated with pain and grief and wondered if it would ever feel like home to her again, especially now that Gram was no longer there and wasn't coming back. Daniela knew the answer to that question as soon as she stepped inside the house and sensed the same hollow and empty feeling that'd pervaded her spirit earlier. That was when she decided she needed to return to Charlotte, which meant facing her fears, but also trusting God who provides hope for the future.

Chapter 35

The evidence of change was as dramatic as crossing over from death to life. In Daniela's case, Micah witnessed a slow revival of her spirit whenever they spoke by phone. She was more willing to share her feelings with him, which meant they were growing closer despite the physical distance between them. He'd been certain that the separation would cause a rift between them and ruin their chance for a meaningful relationship, but surprisingly, their connection was building steadily.

They spoke about the things that mattered to them the most, and each was grateful to have the other to confide in. In a recent conversation, Daniela told Micah about her greatest regret.

"I regret not knowing what it's like to have a real relationship with my father." She sighed. "That's why we need to make things right with the people in our lives before it's too late."

Micah pondered his own relationship with his family, particularly his father, and felt convicted. "Are you trying to tell me something?" he said half-joking.

"I guess I am, sweetheart," she said quietly. "I'll never get a chance to rebuild the relationship with my father, at least not on this side of eternity. You know how the story ended for us. But the pages are still being written for you and your father and the rest of your family. So please don't let it be too late."

Micah happily reported that he and Mark were on speaking terms again. "He actually came to visit me and we had a nice talk. Since then we've been keeping in touch."

"That's good news," Daniela said with a smile in her voice. "How did that happen?"

Then they both said uniformly, "It has God's handprint all over it."

And they laughed.

"He can do the same with your father, you know."

"That's a harder nut to crack," Micah said wryly. "But I'm willing to try."

"I'm glad."

After a slight pause, Micah broached the topic of her return, which she'd informed him she was going to do, but hadn't set a date yet. "I hope it's soon. I really miss having you near me."

"I miss you too, Micah," she said. "It'll be soon, I promise."

Daniela sat down on the padded stall of a local bridal shop inside of a busy strip mall in Miami waiting patiently for Therese to emerge from the fitting room in yet another one of the wedding gowns on display.

Smiling, she shook her head as she surveyed the various dresses on the cramped racks. For the first time she started to wonder if this could be her reality also. After her parents' tragic marriage and her own limited experiences with men, she'd given up on the prospect of getting married a long time ago. But her heart was being changed and so was her mind; and it had to do with Micah, the only man who made her wish for this path that she'd been so fearful to take. God had crossed their paths, which was a journey that they were trudging together, pushing forward with interlocked arms.

Daniela turned in time to see Therese walking toward her wearing a white off-the-shoulder, A-line, sequined gown.

"That one looks good on you," she remarked as she stood to survey the dress up close.

"But it's too plain," Therese whined. "It's not me at all."

Daniela agreed. "Then go try on another one."

Therese shook her head. "This is the last one for the day. I'm tired and I know you are too."

Daniela couldn't argue with that, since they'd been shopping for the better part of the morning. As they exited the store, she placed a comforting hand on her cousin's back.

"It's still early in the game. You'll find the right dress, don't worry."

They got inside of Therese's car, and she drove out of the strip mall, nodding and sighing. "I hope so," she said. "You know how compulsive I get about getting things done and on time."

"Why don't you let your mom give you some input," Daniela offered. "Aunt Sylvie has really good taste."

Therese shook her head adamantly. "No way! I have banned my mom from having any say in the dress I choose. Can you believe she wants to pay some seamstress I know nothing about to make an original dress for me?"

Daniela laughed. "Okay, maybe that's not such a good idea."

Therese continued lamenting over her dress as she pulled into the parking lot of a Haitian restaurant they used to visit on a regular basis before Daniela moved away.

"I haven't been to Chez Millot's in years," Daniela said as they descended the car. "Do they still have the best Haitian food in town?"

"It's because of this place I have to lose all this weight before the wedding."

Daniela shook her head, smiling as they entered the quaint, box-shaped restaurant. Immediately she was transported back in time. Most of the furniture was made out of bamboo wood, and there were various Haitian art and décor pieces displayed on the walls and throughout the restaurant. The Haitian flag was encased in a frame and placed above the checkout area. She smiled to herself as they sat down at a table near the storefront window. They were looking at the menu when Therese's phone rang.

Daniela stood up and circled around the restaurant to give her cousin time to speak with her fiancé, Malcolm. She stood in front of an art piece that displayed a man, woman, and child standing near a small shack. The man and woman were staring at the child who was playing with a butterfly. The picture brought tears to her eyes, and she was unaware of them until Therese came to stand beside her.

"I'm all right," she said in response to her cousin's inquiry.

Temporarily forgetting her sadness, she allowed Therese to steer her back to their table. The waitress came over and they placed their orders. Therese ordered the rice and beans with fried pork and pressed plantains; and Daniela decided on the cornmeal and stewed vegetables with beef. For desert they both decided to have a slice of sweet potato pie.

Once they'd received their meals and said grace, Therese peered at her. "I saw you staring up at that picture. It reminds you of the past, right?"

She glanced down at her plate and nodded slightly. She knew that if she looked into her cousin's empathetic eyes she'd tear up.

"I'm sorry, Dani. I know things are hard for you right now."

Clearing her throat, Daniela looked up and tried to smile. "I'd rather be talking about your upcoming wedding and this wedding dress dilemma."

Therese smiled and took a bite of her food. "Enough about me and this wedding dress fiasco. Tell me what you're going to do now. Are you going to stick around for a bit longer or head back to Charlotte?"

She picked at her plate with her fork. "I do plan on going back to Charlotte. But there are a few things I need to put in order here first before I go, like figuring out what to do about my Dad's house." Then she peered at her cousin intently as a thought crossed her mind. "Tess, have you and Malcolm decided on a place to stay after you get married? If you haven't, I know of this great and very affordable starter home that would be perfect for the two of you."

Therese squinted at her thoughtfully as she dabbed at her mouth with her napkin. "I think it's a good idea. Let me talk to him about it, okay?" she said. "If I get my way we'll soon be your new tenants."

Chapter 36

Daniela drew comfort from members of her old church when she attended the nightly service. She'd thirsted for God's Word and was satiated with the sermon the pastor preached about determining God's will for one's life.

"God's will is not about you, but all about Him. Submit yourself and He will use you to do mighty things for His glory."

Daniela returned home with newfound determination to follow the path she was certain God was leading her. She realized that His desire for her involved more than she would have ever hoped or dreamed as new ideas circulated around in her mind. When she spoke with Micah that evening, she was eager to share a new vision with him.

"I think we can do so much more than we think we can do," she said with excitement. "I have so many things I want to accomplish in the community."

"Yeah, there's no excuse. We've been equipped to do good works, right?" Micah said, smiling.

"Well, look who's been reading up on his Bible."

"I'm just trying to keep up with my lady." They laughed.

Daniela could see the evidence of Micah's journey back to the faith. He willingly shared with her how God had given him the vision to start his business, which had helped thousands of blind people lead more productive lives.

"You're all packed for next week?" he asked her. "I can't wait till you get here."

"Me too," she said. "I'm almost wrapped up here, especially since I finally took care of the matter concerning what to do with Dad's house."

"What did you decide to do?"

Daniela told Micah about renting the house to her cousin instead of selling it. "That way the house will remain in the family and I know it will be taken care of," she concluded.

"That's very smart thinking."

"Now it's your turn. Tell me how things are going with you?"

"Things are going well with the business; sales have gone up for the Can-Do-Cane since its distribution less than one month ago."

"That's wonderful news," Daniela said with excitement.

"And as far as the family ties go, things are slowly improving."

"It won't happen overnight," she said.

"But I'm glad to be making the effort," he said. "It took a conversation with a wise woman to show me that I needed to make amends if I didn't want to live with regrets."

"Anyone I know?" she asked, smiling.

"Not unless you know this woman named Victoria," he said playfully. "A pretty lady whose been checking a brother out."

"Hey, that better be a joke, Mr. Lambert."

Micah chuckled. "You know you're the only one for me."

Daniela sighed contentedly. "And you're the man of my dreams."

"That's music to my ears. But for real, I'm glad you're doing better, baby," Micah said. "Now what I'm hoping is to have you here with me in person instead of being miles away."

"Me too, sweetheart," Daniela echoed softly. "We'll be together again before you know it."

"Good," he said. "I'll be waiting."

Chapter 37

Daniela got off the plane at the international airport in Charlotte, and looked around at the countless number of people who were either coming back to or going away from the city. And though she tried to deflect that feeling of uncertainty which had been pervading her spirit ever since she'd made the decision to return, it was now lording over her and making her want to run back in the direction of those who were going elsewhere. But she forced herself to keep moving forward, with each step drawing her closer to a reunion with Micah.

Daniela smoothed down her brown tinged terra cotta blouse and dark blue jeans and patted down her growing afro. As she exited the terminal she was met with the warmth and brightness of the sun which evidenced the onset of spring and the departure of winter. She glanced around for signs of Micah. The sidewalk was milling about with passengers, and she tried to sift through the crowd. It wasn't long before she spotted him in the background, standing in front of the limo and patiently waiting for her as he promised he would.

Daniela realized once again just how handsome Micah was with his golden brown complexion, even features, and the unique specks of freckles on his face. But more than his appearance it was his kindness and sincerity, along with his caring and gentle nature, that'd captured her heart. She made her way toward him.

"Hi, Micah. I'm here," she said.

He stretched out his arms and she stepped into his embrace, certain that he could feel the thumping of her heart.

"I've missed you," he whispered in her ear.

"I've missed you, too."

Micah smiled. "Let's get you home," he said once they'd parted.

Inside the limo, Micah sought her hand and drew her closer to him. Daniela yielded and they sat closely together.

"So how does it feel to be back?"

"It feels right," she said, glancing down at their linked hands. "Like this is where I'm supposed to be."

"That's what I was hoping you'd say." Micah chuckled.

Daniela caressed his cheek. "I couldn't have pulled through this terrible trial without you," she said.

He took hold of her hand and kissed the nape of her palm. "If it's up to me you'll never have to face another trial alone again. I'd like to take you out to dinner tonight after you've settled in. There's something I'd like to talk to you about."

Daniela squinted in her seat and glanced at his serious expression. He was hinting at a level of commitment she was not certain she was ready to make.

Speaking with more enthusiasm than she felt, she said, "Dinner sounds great."

Daniela didn't know what to wear for her evening dinner date with Micah, and she tried on several outfits before settling on a formal cream-colored pantsuit which she wore with an emerald green silk blouse. She took some time to apply her make-up, and then accessorized with an emerald green beaded necklace and matching earrings. Her cream-colored open-toe three-inch heeled pumps completed the outfit.

As the time for Micah to arrive drew near, her palms grew sweaty and her throat grew dry. She went into the kitchen and downed a glass of water. She was nervous about what he wanted to tell her.

When her cell phone rang, she grabbed her belongings and went down to meet Micah. She slid into the backseat of the car next to him and couldn't help but to be impressed by his appearance. His dress shirt and blazer and dark slacks suited him well.

Apart from greeting him, she was too preoccupied with her thoughts to say anything else and watched the world mutely from her passenger side window.

"I bet you're nervous about tonight," Micah said.

"It's that obvious, huh?" She giggled.

"Yes, it is." He twisted around to face her. "Maybe it'll help to know that I am too."

"Misery loves company, right?"

"Yeah, something like that."

They chuckled as they recalled the words they'd spoken when they'd first sat down together at the deli to talk, which seemed like ages ago. It helped to ease the tension in the air. But Daniela's tenseness soon returned as they reached the restaurant that Micah had picked out. It was a one level, brown building that seemed unassuming on the outside, but was brimming with character on the inside. He asked for her hand and she slipped it inside of his. The warmth radiating from his touch sent ripples of electrical current up her arm and jumpstarted the sudden pounding of her heart.

Chapter 38

Once they'd been seated at a table, the waitress took their orders. When they were left alone, Daniela looked in Micah's direction and tried to denote what he was thinking. He seemed calm, though he had a pensive expression on his face.

"Shall we say grace," he stated, once they'd been served.

They held hands and bent their heads as Micah prayed over the food. But Daniela was too nervous to eat, and she toyed with her food while waiting for Micah to reveal the reason why he wanted to speak with her.

He wiped his mouth with the cloth napkin and took a deep breath. "I know you're wondering why I wanted us to speak tonight, and I won't hold you in suspense any longer." He cleared his throat. "I want you to know that I'm fully committed to our relationship and I want to marry you, Daniela." He put up his hands to halt any comment. "Now, this isn't me proposing, yet. Let's just say it's the proposal before the proposal. I want you to know what my intentions are."

She looked down at her food and saw its blurry image through her unshed tears. "I'm not the best candidate for marriage, Micah." She sniffled. "I don't know if I'm capable of it."

"I know you are," he said intently. "You just have to believe it too."

She sighed. "I know I should have more faith than I do, but I'm afraid that the past will always be the factor that ruins our relationship."

Micah reached for her hands and gripped them firmly. "It doesn't have to be, not if we don't let it," he said. "Can't you see, sweetheart, that we make sense because of our past experiences? God brought us together because He knew we'd connect on a deep level. He knew that we could help each other to find the healing and the love we both needed—"

While Micah was speaking, a woman approached their table and interrupted the conversation.

Claudia had been sitting across from her date, scrutinizing his chiseled, lean frame, his even features, white smile, and the caramel smoothness of his skin and she'd determined that she'd done well to let him take her out. Jeffrey Gibbs, who'd been asking her out repeatedly, was a top-rated attorney who was running for a state representative seat. She was impressed by the level of recognition he was receiving while she was in his company.

While admiring the high-end restaurant that Jeffrey had decided to bring her to, Claudia spotted Micah having dinner with a date and squinted with anger at the familiar-looking tall, lanky woman. Instinctively, she'd gotten up from the table, leaving her bewildered guest behind and had approached them.

Now she greeted them with mock cheerfulness. "What a wonderful surprise."

"Claudia," Micah said in a resigned tone, as though his worst fear had just come true.

"I'm happy to see you too, Micah," she said sarcastically. Then Claudia focused her attention on his dinner guest. "And this must be the mysterious Daniela who I've heard so much about."

She smirked when she saw that Daniela's confused expression morphed into one of recognition.

"You're the woman I met at the supermarket," Daniela said. "You were talking to your friend on the phone about marrying Micah."

"I was more than just talking about it, honey." Claudia snarled and placed her hand on her hip. "I was making it happen until you came into the picture and spoiled everything."

"You need to get a grip on reality, Claudia," Micah interjected firmly.

She tore her eyes away from Daniela and ripped into Micah. "No, sugar, you're the one who needs a reality check. Are you going to deny that we have a relationship, Micah? That we constantly talk on the phone. And that we even had dinner together recently?"

"I can explain," he said to Daniela.

Claudia crossed her arms and watched with satisfaction as Micah squirmed under the heat of her accusation. She crinkled her nose and smiled when she saw the impending tears that were surfacing in Daniela's eyes.

You don't have to explain anything," Daniela said nasally as tears began to flow down her cheeks. "Obviously, you've been lying to me all this time."

"Please, listen to me."

Claudia watched as Daniela gathered her things quickly and shuffled out of the restaurant, trying to ignore the loud whispers that were trailing her from the diners who'd been privy to this private conversation. Ignoring the whispers that were continuing to circulate around them, Claudia took the seat that Daniela had vacated.

"That's too bad, sugar, but don't you worry," she said, smiling. "I'm willing to give you another chance, although I have moved on to bigger and better things. My dinner guest tonight is none other than Jeffrey Gibbs, who will be the next state representative of our district."

Micah shook his head incredulously and his nostrils flared with anger. "I knew you were conniving Claudia, but you're also heartless, too. Please don't do me any favors by giving me another chance, and as far as your dinner guest goes, tell Mr. Gibbs I send him my condolences."

"It looks like the only one mourning is you, sugar, since you can kiss your Daniela goodbye." She giggled mirthlessly and sauntered back to her table and her date.

After he left the restaurant, Micah tried calling Daniela repeatedly but received no answer. He thought about his next course of action as he sat down inside the limo.

"What would you do if you were me?" he asked his limo driver.

"That's easy," Ben said. "I'd go after my blessing."

"What if your blessing doesn't want to be had?" Micah responded dryly. "Maybe this is how it's supposed to end."

"Sir, I think you have a say in how it's supposed to end." Ben cleared his throat. "I think you two make a fine couple, and you should give it your all before you move on."

"You're right, Mr. Ben."

Micah decided to go to Daniela's apartment building and force her to confront him. With his driver's aide, he walked up to her apartment and knocked on the door.

Ben retreated leaving Micah alone to face an angry Daniela. He heard the door swing open. "Come in," she said curtly.

With his cane in hand Micah stepped inside the apartment and stood rigidly near the door while Daniela stood opposite him with her arms folded against her chest.

"You shouldn't have come, Micah. I have nothing to say to you."

"Then I'll talk and you listen," he said. "I didn't lie to you, Daniela. What happened between Claudia and me is in the past, regardless of her claims. And I've made it clear to you that you're the one for me." He lowered his head and sighed. "So don't use what happened tonight as an excuse to run from what we can have together."

She glared at him, but she couldn't muster a rebuttal because she sensed that he was right. "Maybe I'm too afraid of failing to try."

"Then maybe you're not who I thought you were," he said, turning his head away. "Aren't you the same woman who preaches about having faith in God and trusting Him? It's time to practice what you preach and step out on faith and give us a fighting chance."

Her hands fell to her side and she lowered her eyes. "I do know that God can do all things, but it's still so hard to be brave when I've been fearful all of my life."

"I know, sweetheart." Micah took a step toward her. "I'm scared too. But we can't let the fear cripple us and keep us from God's blessings, or are you willing to let the enemy win?"

Daniela's eyes were pooling with tears as she inched toward Micah. "I want God's blessings, and I want us."

"Then fight for us," he said. "Give us a real chance and don't run every time you see a problem. Stay and fight with me."

She nodded in affirmation of his words. "All right, Micah," she said. "I'm tossing out my running shoes for good."

"That's what I was hoping you'd say." He extended his hand toward her, and Daniela walked up to him and placed her hand inside of his.

He drew her close and traced the outline of her face with his hands. She trembled under his perusal. "You're beautiful," he whispered.

"So are you."

Tracing her lips with his thumbs, Micah bent forward and brushed his lips against hers and momentarily took her breath away. And then he drew her into a firm embrace.

Chapter 39

Proudly, Micah gave Daniela a grand tour of the manufacturing site and introduced her to some of his employees, including Ace whom Daniela liked right away. She took it all in like a child who was visiting the fair for the first time. Afterwards, they sat on the large, brown, leather sofa inside of his office with their hands intertwined. She wondered where hers ended and Micah's began.

"I still can't believe you own all of this," Daniela was telling him. "It's incredible. And I'm impressed with the Can-Do-Cane and all the other products that you produce here."

"I wish I could take credit for it, but this is God's doing," he said.

Micah had broached the topic of her coming on board and working in the company, especially since she was no longer working at the library. Though Frances had informed her that her position was still waiting for her if she wanted to return, working for Micah would be more rewarding, both personally and professionally. They'd get a chance to spend more time together, and also he'd provide her with the time and flexibility she needed to do her schoolwork.

"Thank you for wanting me to be a part of it all." She smiled appreciatively.

"I want you to be involved in every area of my life, sweetheart, and I want to be in every aspect of yours," he said. "And I'm looking forward to our future together."

Daniela tried to shrug off the panicky feeling that seemed to come over her each time they discussed the future and marriage. She knew that's what she wanted but it still filled her with a sense of dread. She'd been praying about it fervently in recent days.

"Don't shut down on me now, Daniela," Micah said, reading her like a book. "Tell me what's on your mind."

"I'm still praying to conquer my fears about the future, Micah," she said honestly. She got up from the couch and paced about the floor. "I know it's what I want but it's still hard to ignore the doubts and the fears."

"I hope you don't think I'm rushing you."

She twisted around to face him with her mouth turned downward in a sad expression. "Please, be patient with me, that's all."

"Come here, sweetheart."

Daniela walked back to the couch and sat down beside him. She placed her hands inside of his outstretched palms.

"I'll be as patient as you need me to be, and I'm praying with you and for you," Micah said earnestly. "But I want you to be completely honest with me and with yourself. I want to know that we're aiming for the same thing, which is a life together."

"It is what I want, Micah." She sighed and glanced down at their joined hands. "I just didn't think I'd ever get married or even find the right person to marry until

I met you. Before then, I'd made up my mind that I would remain single and focus on ministry."

"I'm glad that God had other plans." He squeezed her hand.

"Me too," she said and put her head on his shoulder.

They remained in the same position for a short while, enjoying the comfortable silence between them.

Sensing that they were running short on time, Micah said, "We'd better start heading out if we want to make it to the evening service on time."

As they exited the building together, Daniela felt more strongly about the decision she'd made to listen to her heart and to stop running from the man she loved.

Chapter 40

"So have you made a decision on the venue for the reception yet?" Daniela asked Therese over the telephone.

"Yes, we've decided on the banquet hall downtown," she said distractedly. "Dani, please tell me you're coming for your dress fitting."

"Yes, but that's still a few months away."

"I don't want you to forget, that's all. I'd like to stay on schedule. There's too much to do already."

"Tell me what I can do to help."

"I could use your help with choosing the wedding invitations and the wedding favors," Therese said anxiously. "I've narrowed down the choices. I'll send you an email so you can tell me what you think."

"Okay, no problem." Daniela paused and hummed nervously. "I do have a favor to ask you, Tess. Do you think you could add one more person to the guest list?"

"Why? Did I forget someone?"

"I'd like to bring a date, that's all."

"Okay, who is he, and how come I'm only hearing about him now?"

Daniela told Therese about Micah. Her cousin listened in awe, at times voicing exclamations.

"So it doesn't bother you that he's blind?" Therese asked when Daniela had finished her account.

"No it doesn't." She shook her head for emphasis. "The truth is that in many ways I'm the one who's been blind. I'd been so focused on the past I couldn't see that Micah was a part of the divine plan for my future."

"Have you told Gram about your man?"

"Yes, and she's thrilled."

They laughed.

"If you're happy, Dani, then I'm happy for you. And I'd be glad to add Micah's name to the guest list." She giggled. "I told you your big day would come."

"I wouldn't go that far." She thought about the nervous tension that settled in her stomach each time Micah hinted at the subject of marriage. "I know he's the one for me, and he does want to marry me, but I still feel a little shaky about taking the big step. He's being very understanding about it."

"It's good you found someone willing to bear with your hardheadedness," Therese said with a giggle.

"Thanks a lot." Daniela smiled. "I'm getting there. It's just that I still think about my parents and the type of marriage they had and I don't want to live through that again in my own life. It scares me that there's even a small possibility that it can happen."

"All I know is that you can't let fear get in the way of something you really want to do. Isn't that what having faith is about?"

"Yes, I know." She nodded and sighed. "But it's easier to preach it than to do it."

After she got off the phone with her cousin, Daniela became restless. After minutes of standing beside her living room window and staring off into the distance, she grabbed her car keys and left her apartment. She went to the one place where she often sought peace.

Several minutes later she was entering the empty sanctuary at Bethel Baptist Church. She took her place at her usual pew and immediately felt the tears trickling down her face as she sought God's presence. She picked up her Bible and hugged it against her chest.

"Lord, please help me," she mouthed. The turmoil in her heart caused her to double over in her seat. She gripped the back of the pew in front of her. "Lord, You say in Your Word that nothing is impossible to them that believe. So please help me to believe that marriage is possible, since You've supplied me with a good, godly man to share my life with. Help me to overcome the fear of repeating the mistakes of my parents."

Chapter 41

Daniela's favorite times were the ones she spent with Micah, talking about the deep things of life that made their relationship as treasured as a pearl nestled inside of an oyster. Right now, Daniela sat with him in the park that he loved so much and she huddled close to him and felt his soothing arm draped around her shoulder.

"I have to tell you something, sweetheart," he said.

She looked up at his face, which bore a sober expression and waited for him to speak.

"I can see now," he said simply.

"What?" Daniela pulled away from him and looked searchingly at his closed eyelids.

Micah smiled. "I don't mean physically, baby, although I know that God can do that too if He wants to." He paused and tilted his head toward the bluish sky. Then he turned in her direction. "All this time, I've been blaming God for being blind, Daniela. And I fought against it, and I wanted to beat it so bad and I thought I could do that by amassing all this success and getting all these accolades to show that I made it even with this wretched condition dogging me."

Daniela leaned against Micah once more, listening intently to his words and stroking his hand comfortingly.

"But all this time, I couldn't see that God has been with me through it all. And that He allowed this bad thing to happen to me so that He could cause great things to happen from it for my good and for His glory." Micah shook his head in awe. "Out of my circumstance, He's blessed me both professionally and personally."

Smiling, Daniela nodded, sniffling from the emotions of the moment. "You can see now, can't you? The spiritual eyes are so much more important than the physical ones."

"Yes. He's forgiven me for my stubborn pride." Micah stroked her shoulder tenderly. "And that's why I need to do the same for someone else in my life."

"Your father?" she said perceptively.

"You got it. I've made plans with Mom to go and see him and talk to him, and hopefully give our relationship a fresh start."

"That's a good idea," Daniela said. "I wish I could go with you to offer you some moral support, honey."

"I wish you could too." He placed a light kiss atop Daniela's forehead.

"It'll be all right because God's got your back," she said. "He's in control and it'll work out the way He wants it to."

"I know it will."

Micah thought about Daniela's words as he took the long trip to his parent's estate to speak with his father. Though he didn't know what the outcome of the meeting with his father would be, he did know that regardless of what happened, the fact that they were going to speak at all was a miracle. He pondered what he should say to him. But the words he came up with in his mind sounded contrived and rehearsed, so he decided to just let the conversation take its own course and hopefully reach the desired destination of forgiveness.

He leaned back against the seat and placed his head atop the headrest. A vision of his father came to mind, the man he'd once known and loved. His father was tall, big, and strong. Micah looked up to him. But as the scene progressed, his father's physical stature diminished and he became ordinary. Micah shook his head and rubbed his face, the painful lesson of that image hit him all at once. He'd idolized his father and had thought that the older man could do no wrong. And when his father did let him down, Micah couldn't take the crushing blow. So his disappearance act was as much his fault as it was his father's or anyone else in his family.

"Thank you for showing me the error of my ways," he prayed silently. "I've wasted so much time being angry but You never gave up on me. Now please give me the faith to not give up on a relationship with my father."

He sat up when his driver pulled up to his parent's house. He took a deep breath to quiet his anxiety and got out of the car. With his cane guiding the way, he walked up to the front door. His mother was already there waiting to greet him. No longer hindered by bitterness and time, Micah hugged her warmly and smiled.

"Thanks for setting this up, Mom."

"I want nothing more than for the two of you to work things out," she said.

Ann Lee circled her arms around her son's arm and led him to the study where his father was waiting. Then she left them alone and closed the door behind her.

The ensuing silence was deafening. Micah shifted in the leather couch where he sat. He could smell the strong sent of pine and polish. His father's study had always been impressive, including the walled bookcase that was stocked with books that'd take a lifetime to read.

"I remember how much you loved to read and to study, Dad." He spoke up. "This room has always been your sanctuary."

"It still is," Morris Lambert affirmed.

Micah leaned forward and placed his elbows on his knees. He lowered his head slightly and then proceeded to say the first words that came to mind. "I'm here because I want us to be on speaking terms again," he said. "I know you're angry with me and maybe you always will be, but that doesn't mean we have to be enemies."

His father didn't speak, and Micah sat and waited. He'd extended the peace offering and it was up to his father to accept it.

"So I'm supposed to forget about the seventeen years that you walked out on your family."

"Yes, Dad," he said pointedly, "just like I've opted to forget about the seventeen years my family's abandoned me."

"What do you mean we abandoned you?"

"I didn't travel very far, Dad," he responded. "You could've easily gotten in touch with me if you'd wanted to. The truth is, you wanted to keep your distance because you were ashamed of me."

A loud silence settled between them like a large gulf that seemed impossible to cross.

His father sighed heavily. "We weren't prepared for what'd happened to you, Micah." His tone was a shell of its prior conviction and indignation. "We didn't know how to handle the disability. But we were never ashamed of you."

Micah turned his head toward the floor to ceiling window in the study. "That's how I felt, Dad, like someone who'd been thrown away in a reject pile and was designated a lost cause."

"So you thought the best way to handle things was to leave?" his father asked flatly.

Micah bowed his head. "I know I handled things wrong. And I can't go back and change it." He spoke hoarsely, his feelings raw and exposed. "But I'd like us to move past it and consider a fresh start. Do you think we can, Dad?"

Morris Lambert paused. "Why now, after all these years?"

"Because God has given us this time, and I don't want to miss out on the opportunity to make amends."

"I don't want to be angry anymore," his father uttered with unshed tears in his eyes as he watched his son.

"Me neither, Dad," Micah said. He stood up and stretched out his hand and waited for his father to shake it.

Morris Lambert got up from his desk chair across the room and trekked toward his son, closing the wide distance that separated them. He gripped the hand that

Micah was extending and then pulled his son into a firm embrace.

"I'm sorry, son. I never meant to make you feel ashamed."

Micah returned his father's embrace and silently thanked God for yet another miracle.

Chapter 42

Though Daniela had resumed her attendance and participation at Bethel Baptist Church, she still felt uneasy when she thought about Mason Goodwin and his strong opinions against her preaching, which he sought to propagate in the church. In an attempt to stop the problem before it went any further Daniela set up a meeting with Pastor Sanders and relayed the troublesome conversation she'd had with the young pastor before she left for Florida.

She was surprised at Pastor Sanders' reaction to her revelation. "He tried to get me to turn against you, too," Pastor Sanders revealed gravely. "When I failed to listen, he made it known that he refused to partake in a ministry that allowed women to assume positions that are due men. And you know what I said?" Pastor Sanders leaned forward in his chair conspiratorially, with a mischievous grin on his face. "Good riddance."

He and Daniela shared a laugh and immediately she felt at ease once more in her church home. She went home praising the Lord for His faithfulness.

Now Daniela was humming softly to herself as she moved about in her kitchen preparing a home-cooked meal for herself and Micah that she hoped he'd enjoy. He'd arrived a little earlier and was now sitting in the living room, listening to her and smiling.

"I could listen to you all day," he said in amusement.

She smiled. "I'm still thinking about the meeting I had with Pastor Sanders and how God turned the situation around. He truly can make all things work together for our good and for His glory."

Micah didn't say anything for a moment. "He certainly can, even in matters of the heart."

Daniela stopped mid-motion and gazed up at him, knowing exactly what he was referring to. Her cold heart had melted and now it was filled with love for the man who was sitting in her living room and waiting patiently for her. Slowly, she rinsed and toweled off her hands and went to join him on the couch. Micah shifted to face her.

Though they'd agreed to stave off the topic of marriage for a time, it still hung in the air between them like smog. She continued to remain in prayer about it. She's also been in counseling with Rebecca James, a Christian counselor whom Pastor Sanders had recommended she speak with. Rebecca had been taking her through the Word of God and showing her the beauty of this sacred union that God had instituted. Seeing it from a godly perspective was making all the difference in the world.

Like Rebecca told her in a recent counseling session, "When it's done God's way, it's a beautiful thing."

Daniela took hold of Micah's hand. "I'm not afraid anymore, Micah. I want our future together, and I'm ready to discuss it with you."

"I'm glad to hear you say that." Micah cleared his throat as he slid down off the couch and got down on one knee. "I wasn't prepped for this so I don't have a ring to present to you. But I don't want this opportunity to go by without making it official. Sweetheart, will you marry me?"

She threw her arms around his neck. "I would love to marry you."

He belted out a merry laugh as he circled his arms around her. Standing, they held each other tightly and he kissed her tenderly on the lips.

"I promise before God to be the best husband I can be for you, Daniela," he whispered.

"And I will prayerfully be the wife that God wants me to be for you."

She bumped him playfully. "Now let me get back to my cooking so that I can feed my future husband."

Micah chuckled. "I like the sound of that."

Epilogue

Daniela shot up out of bed as reality dawned on her—today was her wedding day. She rushed to the bathroom to get ready for an early breakfast with her small wedding party to unwind before beginning preparations for the wedding.

As she sat down at the restaurant with Therese, her matron of honor, who had come to Charlotte for the wedding, and her two bridesmaids, Frances and Jackie, she tried to cover up the unsettling feeling in her stomach.

"What's wrong, Dani? You haven't touched your food," Therese commented.

She turned away, trying to hide the tears that were brimming to the surface of her eyes. The table became silent and Daniela noticed the looks of concern on their faces.

"I'm okay," she said unconvincingly.

"Don't you want to get married, Dani?" Frances asked.

"I thought you and Brother Micah were a match made in heaven," Jackie added.

"I know I want to marry Micah, and that he's the one for me. I just hope that I'll be a good wife to him." She shrugged.

Therese reached out and touched her hand, giving it a supportive squeeze. "You will make a great wife," she said. "Don't get me wrong, marriage is hard work."

"How would you know, Ms. Six-months married?" Daniela teased.

"I know that Malcolm is not as clean as he pretended to be before we were married," Therese mouthed tersely. "I'm already tired of having to clean up after him all the time."

"Marriage is hard, y'all," Jackie piped in. "I've been married for 15 years and sometimes I still wonder why—"

They all turned to look at Jackie with stricken expressions on their faces.

"Sorry," Jackie said sheepishly. "I guess that's not helping right about now."

"No, not helping," Frances shook her head.

They all laughed and Daniela felt less tense and more at ease.

Two hours later Daniela stood in front of the full length mirror staring at her reflection and trying to contain her tears, which were joyous ones this time. Who was this woman dressed in white, made up to perfection, and waiting to be joined to her chosen mate in holy matrimony? She was no longer the woman who was an island unto herself; but rather, she was now connecting to her future husband, mind, body, and spirit.

When the time came, Daniela stood outside the door of the sanctuary of Bethel Baptist Church, waiting to walk down the aisle. She gripped the arm of her soon-to-be father-in-law, Morris Lambert, who had kindly offered to walk her down the aisle, and she'd gratefully accepted.

The wedding processional ensued, and soon they were making their way down the aisle. Daniela spotted the people she cared about looking at her with such love in their eyes, including her grandmother, and she broke down. Then her gaze was riveted on Micah and her earlier concerns faded away. She smiled with thankfulness as she spotted his brother, Mark, his best man, giving him an affectionate pat on his shoulder as he smiled approvingly in her direction.

Once they were standing side by side, Pastor Sanders, who was presiding over the wedding, had them face one another to recite their personal vows, and then officially pronounced them as husband and wife. Daniela's heart soared. She felt like she had won the fight over her fears by believing in the hope and the future that God had designed for her life and not in the lie that her past was her future.

They kissed each other tenderly.

"I love you, Mrs. Lambert," Micah whispered against her ear.

"I love you, Mr. Lambert," she whispered back.

Acknowledgements

I thank my heavenly Father, who has given me this opportunity to share this story with others.

I'd also like to thank all of my family and friends who have been and continue to be a source of strength and support. Thank you and I love you all.

I'd like to express my appreciation to Dr. A'ndrea J. Wilson and Divine Garden Press for coming alongside me and making this dream a reality.

To the Readers, thank you for giving this book a chance. I pray it speaks to you and says what God wants it to say.

Blessings,

Irvine Saint-Vilus

Reading Group Guide

1. Why do you think Micah felt so strongly about Daniela after meeting her for the first time? Do you think this encounter was realistic? Why or why not?
2. What personal characteristics and experiences do Micah and Daniela share that unite them and help to build their relationship?
3. Do you consider the past a main character in the story? How does it impact the lives of Micah and Daniela? Scripture says, "And we know that in all things God works for the good of those who love Him, and who have been called according to His purpose" (Rom. 8:28 NIV). Should someone regret his or her past if God uses it to help the person to become who he or she was meant to be?
4. In chapter 14 Daniela struggles with doubts about her calling because of the opinions of others. Was there a time in your life that you decided not to do something because other people thought that you couldn't do it? What was the result of your decision?
5. Why do you think it is so difficult for Micah and Daniela to forgive their loved ones? Is forgiveness a simple act or a process that requires time and patience for it to occur?
6. Why is it so important to Micah to trust others and to have others trust him, especially in his

relationship with Daniela? What does Micah do to build trust in his relationship with Daniela?

7. On different occasions Daniela is prepared to walk away from her relationship with Micah, especially after meeting Claudia. Why do you think she is prepared to give up so easily?

8. In the story, Daniela seeks ways to witness to her friend, Frances. Do you think this is a realistic portrayal of sharing the gospel with friends and family? If not, how can Christians be effective witnesses when it comes to telling others about Jesus?

9. In chapter 39, Daniela's fears about marriage are emphasized. Why is Daniela so afraid of getting married if she is already certain that Micah is the man that God has given to her as her lifetime partner? Is her fear reasonable or unwarranted?

10. At the conclusion of the story, Micah and Daniela are married. Also, Micah was able to reconcile with his brother and father. How should a Christian novel end, happily or realistically, which does not always produce happy results?

Resources

In this story, we are confronted with the serious issue of domestic violence, which continues to plague our society today. As the story also demonstrates, children are adversely affected by domestic violence. We must make a concerted effort to end the violence against women and to stop exposing the violence to our children. If you or anyone you know is being abused, or if you would like to help, the following is a list of resources to go to for more information:

Safe Horizon: 1-800-621-HOPE (4673)
www.safehorizon.org

The National Domestic Violence Hotline: 1-800-799-7233
www.thehotline.org

Domestic Violence Prevention Center: 1-888-528-1041
www.ywca.org

About the Author

Irvine Saint-Vilus is the author of the faith-based novels *Even Me* and *Running from My Life*. She enjoys writing Christian fiction stories that address serious societal issues. Irvine received a Bachelor's degree in English at the University of North Carolina at Charlotte and a Master's degree in Divinity at Liberty University in Lynchburg, Virginia. She currently resides in Lynchburg where she works in the public school system and is involved in ministry activities.

VISIT
WWW.DIVINEGARDENPRESS.COM
FOR OTHER GREAT TITLES!